THE ART OF LOVE

Dangerous Love Book One

JOY BUSSU

Published by Blushing Books
An Imprint of
ABCD Graphics and Design, Inc.
A Virginia Corporation
977 Seminole Trail #233
Charlottesville, VA 22901

Joy Bussu
The Art of Love

eBook ISBN: 978-1-64563-951-0
Print ISBN: 978-1-64563-952-7
v1

Prologue

She noticed him the minute he entered the VIP section. His group of tables were directly next to hers. Gold bottles of 'Ace of Spades' champagne were gripped in the hands of his crew. Scantily clad women on their laps going along for the free ride. He sat back quietly observing it all but not engaging in any of the activities.

Every so often he would lean forward and conduct business in the middle of it all. His butterscotch-hued skin reflected the colors of the strobe lights in crazy shades.

He glanced in her direction and lifted his glass before taking a sip. She smiled when the waitress brought a glass containing the same liquid to her.

She lifted the glass in his direction and pretended to take a drink. She never drank more than a few glasses of white wine and never in public settings like this. If things were to take a turn for the worse, she needed a clear head.

Her own crew carried themselves differently, no popping bottles or making it rain. All female, all classy, all the wrong bitches to fuck with.

Her second in command and best friend, Yolan, leaned

over nudging her. "I saw that," she teased, casting a gaze at the man in the other VIP section.

"Yolan, don't start and don't lose focus. We are here for one reason and one reason only," Tayana reminded her and stared at the dance floor below. She had four of her crew mingling down there, keeping an eye out.

"Yeah, yeah, Tay, I know. Quiet moves are successful moves." Yolan shook her head and poured more champagne in her now empty glass. "One day, Tay, you are going to have to let your hair down. I mean, Thirst was three years ago. Ain't it past time to move on from his treacherous ass?" Yolan continued, trying to reason with her best friend, who was too damn pretty and had too much going for her to be single forever.

Tayana's eyes narrowed in Yolan's direction. Yolan was the only one who could bring him up and not catch a beat down, and she knew it. "I don't control the universe, Yo. When it's time to move on, I will move on. Now drop it, please. Shay is onto something."

Her girl Shay could have been a model. She was as deadly as she was beautiful and for that reason, she was very valuable to Tayana.

Tayana caught eyes with Shay and followed her glance. There they were, the only reason she bothered to come to this pit of a club, Raz and Jammy, short for Jamaica. Tayana winked at Shay to confirm she needed to grab Monet and work them.

She saw movement out of the corner of her eye and noticed *he* was now standing to shake the wrinkles out of his slacks. Tall, at least 6'5", just like she liked them. Judging by his wavy fade and high cheekbones he was most definitely mixed with something. Her one weakness was a pretty man and after Thirst's double-crossing ass, she was cool on them all but couldn't help looking when one crossed her path.

"Yo, Tay, where you at?" Yolan nudged her again and motioned her head towards the dance floor.

She immediately returned her glance to her ladies below. Shay and Monet were out front, directly in their line of sight, Khyrs and Jaidyn were mingling in the crowd, being invisible as only her ladies could be. Pretty? Yes, all of her ladies were but she made them dress down so they didn't stand out. Jammy was slowly walking over to Monet, a drink in each hand. Raz was leaning on the bar watching Shay dance and slow wind. She made it a point to stay in his line of vision using the man she was dancing with as her prop, her focus stayed on Raz. If he didn't bite, this wouldn't work.

Yolan signaled to Monet. She knew not to reel Jammy all the way in until Shay had Raz under her spell. Now it was just a waiting game.

Tayana risked a glance over at the other VIP area when the sound of guns cocking in her own VIP area caught her attention. Her bodyguards Rini and Joy were now standing at the entrance of their circle of tables blocking *him* from moving any closer to her.

To the untrained eye they just appeared to be having a friendly conversation, but she knew her ladies. Their hidden guns weren't just for show. He, however, looked unfazed and undeterred. *Bold, that can be both a blessing and a curse,* Tayana noted to herself.

"Shit, what the hell?" Yolan whispered, fiercely looking over her shoulder, annoyed with the distraction *he* was causing.

"Focus, Yo. Looks like Raz is biting. I will handle this."

Tayana caught Rini's eye who un-cocked her gun and moved to let him through. Joy, the only real hot head in the crew, followed closely behind him over to Tayana, gun still ready to sing.

His cologne introduced him a few moments before he was

standing in front of her, looking like her damn fantasies come to life.

Tayana sat back and crossed her legs. Her Dior mini dress slid up a little bit exposing more of her thighs, which he immediately noticed. He licked his lips as he stared at her exposed skin.

"*Ahem*, can I help you?" Tayana asked, throwing him a lot of attitude. Pretty or not, this muthafucka was interfering with her business.

He slid into the seat next to her and smiled over at her. "My apologies, I just wanted to come over and introduce myself. I know everyone in this city but I don't remember ever meeting you. Name's Jazz, and yours, Boss Lady?" He extended his hand to her.

Tayana caught Yolan's glance and lifted her eyebrow just before smiling sweetly. "My given name is Tayana, you can call me Whisper like everybody else does, and you have about five seconds to cut the shit and speak your mind before things get ugly in VIP."

Tayana took his hand in her own, flashing him a venomous smile. Her breath caught for a millisecond from their contact, she quickly pushed the feeling away, now was not the time or place for this type of shit!

Jazz's eyes met hers for a brief moment before he cleared his throat. Obviously, he felt it too. "Well, damn, like that? I see you, Whisper. Anyway, I came over to ask, as a professional courtesy, to step back this time."

Catching his meaning Tayana glanced down at the dance floor, seems Raz and Jammy had more than one enemy in attendance tonight. Noting all four of her girls and Raz and Jammy were no longer visible, she looked over at Yolan for confirmation. Her smile told her all she needed to know.

"Unfortunately, Jazz, you're a little too late with your request, but I can pass along a message if you like." Tayana smiled again and picked up the drink he had sent over earlier and took a sip.

Cognac, expensive cognac. If she had to guess she would say *Tesseron Extreme*. Her mother taught her well, she made sure Tayana had a taste of the finer things, how to know the real from the fake on sight or taste. Tayana could spot the best of the best knockoffs as soon as she laid eyes on it.

Nothing about Jazz was fake, especially the deadly glare he was sending her way, now that she had shot him and his request down.

"Hmm, that's unfortunate. I was hoping we could come to a compromise." Jazz boldly took the glass from Tayana's hand and took a drink, watching her with his light eyes the entire time.

If she was ever inclined to come out of retirement and date again, Jazz would most definitely be the type of man she would want to start with. His boldness and confidence seemed to exude from his pores.

"Well, Jazz, that was your first mistake. I never compromise. It implies indecision, weakness. Now, if there is nothing else to discuss, I would like to get back to minding my business, please." Tayana snatched back her glass and tossed back the remaining cognac.

Jazz's fine ass had her breaking her own rules already, not good!

"Hmm, Boss Lady has teeth. I like that. Yeah we will most definitely have more to discuss at another time. Good night, Whisper."

Jazz stood up and shook the wrinkles out of his Dolce slacks. *Clothes whore.* Tayana smiled knowingly to herself. Everyone has a weakness and with that little habit of his, he exposed one of his.

"Good night, Jazz. Thank you for the drink," Tayana stated, fighting to ignore how his professionally tailored slacks cupped his bulge, the man was blessed in more ways than one!

He smiled down at her, his gaze running from the top of her head to her manicured toes that were being cradled by her gold Louboutin's.

"Anytime." He turned on his heel, to return to his own VIP and crew.

Joy followed him until he was out of their area, finally uncocking her gun and settling back in her seat at the entrance of their circle of tables.

"So what do you think that was about?" Yolan asked, while watching Jazz who was settling back into the seat he had vacated and was now having a conversation with one of the men sitting closest to him. Once he finished, he glanced over his shoulder in Tay's direction and winked. She smiled a flirty smile and focused her attention back onto Yolan.

"Oh, Yo, you already know, curiosity, plain and simple." Tayana's phone vibrated, she accepted the call and held it to her ear silently.

"It's done," she said before hanging up.

"We are playing with the big boys now, remember, Yo? And what's the one thing I told you they all hate about our crew?" Tayana asked, pouring herself a little club soda to dilute the cognac she drank.

Yolan shrugged, still watching Jazz looking annoyed. "What?"

"That the crew with no dicks is proving to have the biggest dicks of all."

Chapter 1

J azz stepped into his walk-in shower and turned all four heads on full blast, something he always did when he was deep in thought, times like now. He was still intrigued, impressed and yes, a little annoyed by Tayana aka Whisper and her all-female crew.

They swooped in and hit Raz and Jammy so quick, no one had a clue it had even happened until she pointed out to him that it was too late to call her ladies off. Her attitude left a bit to be desired, no one talked to him the way she did but something about it most definitely turned him on. He'd heard mention of her and her ladies more than a few times and to simply ignore them, as he had done up until now, would be foolish.

After witnessing how she and her crew operated, he needed her to know how he worked and because the way his hormones had been buzzing since their hands touched, he needed to know more about her, period.

Tayana's eyes popped open a few seconds before her alarm went off as they always did. She was never one to sleep in, every minute she wasted in bed was a minute she could never get back and she was about making them all count.

She learned early on in her line of business, women were never taken as seriously as the men unless they were made to. Which, in turn, meant she was always on time, always ready for whatever came her way, and so were her ladies.

Slowly, but surely, those men who had once scoffed and blew her and her crew off were recognizing what they were bringing to the party and, like it or not, they had to eat what she served. Raz and Jammy just found out the hard way what happens to those who disrespected her or her crew.

Standing under the stinging rain of her shower, she allowed her mind to finally stop running a mile a minute. Jazz's sexy ass eyes lingered on the edges of her mind as soon as the chaos stopped. She could tell, just like others before him, Jazz thought she was weak, that he could bully her because she was a woman. Little did he know, because of her mother, she was raised with the mental strength and resolve of any man, all while being one-hundred-percent woman.

For as long as she could remember, Tayana watched from the sidelines as her father Jason, known in the streets as 'Heavy', tried his best to sculpt her brothers and teach them the business only to receive constant pushback and resistance. Both of her brothers wanted to continue to reap the benefits of Heavy's hard work without actually putting in any work themselves. They were spoiled little rich boys with too many toys.

Tayana was the exact opposite, from the moment her mother told her the truth about her father's 'business', Tayana was watching and waiting for her chance to put in work. Unfortunately, Heavy never took her seriously until it was too late, and now he was the first of many cautionary tales her name came up in.

Her own daddy doubted her, underestimated her strength until she rose above him and her brothers. In the beginning of 'the end' as she called it, she maintained her business in all areas of their city but her daddy's. Then her father got sloppy and his girlfriend fucked up and killed Tayana's mother, Essie in a jealous rage over a one-of-a-kind pair of fur boots. The girlfriend wrongfully assumed he'd bought the boots for her because he'd hid them in her house until Essie's birthday. The girlfriend crept behind Essie and shot her in the back when she saw her out in them.

That's when the gloves came off. Tayana went for the jugular. She took over all his businesses, one by one, and burned his house to the ground with both him and that skanky bitch sealed inside. Her two brothers were spared and given $5M each to start over far away from Texas, which they were more than happy to do. They were never cut out for this life anyway.

After her shower she dressed in a new custom pantsuit designed by Monet and Shay. She transferred her belongs from her beaded bag from the night before to her Birkin bag that matched her pumps perfectly, today's masterpieces were by Brian Atwood and just looking down at them made her smile. Which was part of the reason she was so quick to notice Jazz was a clothes whore, it takes one to know one. She was one of the biggest ones she knew and that's even with Monet and Shay and their love affair with fashion, which was definitely saying something.

Tayana most definitely proudly wore any and every custom piece Shay and Monet made for her but her walk-in closet was about to burst with clothes right off the runways of Italy, Japan, and New York. She even had a personal shopper who traveled all over the world to secure her fashions many times throughout the year, you name an occasion and she had an outfit to wear for it.

"Are you having breakfast here this morning, Whisper?" Ms. Lanie asked Tayana as she descended the steps to leave for her meeting about a half hour later. Her crew had a 9 a.m. meeting and she was a firm believer in 'If you were on time, you were late'.

"No, I'm meeting the ladies for the monthly meeting today, so we are going to grab something to eat afterwards," Tayana told her cook and housekeeper who had been around her for as long as she could remember.

Ms. Lanie used to work for Essie and Heavy, but jumped at the chance when Tayana asked if she would be interested in working for her when she moved out of her parents' house. Tayana had been the only reason Ms. Lanie stayed with their family so long anyway.

"Okay, well let me know what you want for dinner and what time you'll be home, so I can make sure it's done in time. Loving the shoes by the way, you look fierce, honey!" Ms. Lanie told her snapping her fingers, moving back towards the kitchen.

Tayana lifted her foot and moved it from side to side. "Me too, and thank you Ms. Lanie, you know all you have to do is say the word and Shay and Monet will hook you up something phenomenal," Tayana offered, opening the front door to leave.

"Chile, please, where am I going besides to the grocery store?" Ms. Lanie laughed, shaking her head at Tayana.

Tayana shrugged. "Who knows, Ms. Lanie you might meet your glass slipper man in the meat department," Tayana reasoned with a smile.

Ms. Lanie laughed even harder and walked back into the kitchen. Tayana's smile grew brighter at the thought of Ms.

Lanie finding someone to dress up for and walked out the front door, closing it behind her.

"Aww shit, look at you shine!" her chauffeur, Bruise, and only male bodyguard teased as she exited the house.

"Whatever, B, it's just a business suit but you gotta admit Shay and Monet killed it on this one, though!" Tayana moved to enter the car when he opened the door for her and stopped short.

"Ay, B, what the fuck is that?" She motioned to the bouquet of peach roses on her seat and backed away from the car.

"Shit! Joy, we got a problem!" Bruise quickly alerted Rini and Joy through his earpiece, they seemed to come out of nowhere and moved Tayana back inside the house.

"Whisper, we got this, don't trip," Joy promised, deadly serious and rushed back outside leaving Tayana with Rini. The only one of her crew who still called her by her government name was Yolan. She said it was to keep her grounded, to make sure to always remember who she really was.

Her whole house went on lockdown. Flowers for a regular woman were a compliment, a treat. To a woman in her line of business, flowers were the exact opposite, they were a warning and a threat.

Bruise and Joy rushed back into the house a few minutes later.

"All clear. Whisper, that car was detailed yesterday. That must have been when they were slipped in the back seat." Bruise was all business, all playful banter and his smile from earlier were gone.

Joy shook her head in the negative. "Naw, B, those are fresh, one-hour tops. Someone has a death wish. I'm going to check out the cameras to see whose mama needs a black dress." Joy moved down the hall towards the security office.

"Whisper, should we call the rest of the crew, make sure everyone is cool?" Rini asked, watching Joy's retreating back.

"No, they have all checked in this morning like usual but, just to keep Joy calm, let's move today's meeting here. B, would you mind sounding the alarm to get everybody here, please? I will let Ms. Lanie know to get started on breakfast after all."

Bruise pulled out his phone and sent out the coded message that told the ladies to meet at Whisper's house. Once finished, he quietly left to alert the guard station of what had just happened.

Jazz watched the panicked activity from his vantage point with a small, but amused smile on his face. He had to give Tayana props, her security was a well-oiled machine. He barely had time to get back over the rear wall before they locked her place down. Now that he had her attention it was time to put his plan of attack into action. He had his people digging a little deeper into her background to find out all he could about her, most importantly her love life. He wanted to discover the type of men she dated in the past – so he knew what he was up against – because after a sleepless night, with her on his mind for most of it, he'd made a decision. Tayana Bradley was destined to be his, she just didn't know it yet.

"Do we know who did it? I know Raz and Jammy's peeps ain't this bold." Shay poured creamer in her coffee looking ready to kill.

Joy's anger was radiating off of her in waves. She took her job very seriously. No one had ever gotten this close to the house or Tayana before and Tayana could tell she blamed herself.

"Naw that's the thing, the cameras didn't pick up anybody near that car but B, and he never went inside it. Whoever Harry Houdini is he has got a hot one coming, I promise you, Whisper," Joy snapped, playing with a piece of bacon on her plate.

Tayana sighed and took a sip of her juice, looking around at her crew. "Maybe it's like B said, the car was detailed yesterday and maybe someone there got careless and missed them. Joy, send Bruise over to check it out but until then, fire anyone who hasn't been here more than a year just to be safe."

Joy pushed away from the table to handle the business, Rini looked at Tayana and after her nod, she followed after Joy.

Yolan sitting at her right whistled slowly. "Joy is pissed. You do realize if she figures out who did this she will probably kill their whole family for generations to come right?"

Tayana shook away that image and took a bite of her own slice of bacon. "Anyway, on to business. Shay and Monet, good work as usual. Hope it wasn't too hard to do once you left the club?" she asked looking over at them.

Monet's mouth was full of waffle, so Shay answered, "You know how we do, Whisper, had them dope boys eating outta our hands, never saw it coming. Bet H-Town crew will think twice before disrespecting us again."

"Good to hear. Like I keep telling you all, chances are for suckas. Raz and Jammy got cocky, saw a bunch of beautiful women running shit and thought they could use their dicks to get over on us. No one steals from us and if they do they never live to celebrate the spoils. We don't make a lot of noise and make a production about it, we just plan and take care of business. Ladies, we are always going to be moving targets, never forget that.

"As long as we are holding down the game the way we do, we are a threat. So make your moves, run the businesses, keep focused, but most of all keep quiet. Men are boasters by nature; they have to peacock, one up each other to see whose dick is bigger.

"I know how females are portrayed, especially women of color. Like we are poised and ready to betray our best friend for some dick, or a few measly dollars, or something petty like that. But the reason why we work is because we are above all of that. We have been the best of friends since preschool or longer and we respect what each one of us brings to the table because, at the end of the day, we are all eating."

Tayana signaled for Ms. Lanie to start clearing the table as they all stood to move to the office.

Chapter 2

Tayana took her place at the head of the large oval table in the office. She watched quietly as all of her ladies took their favorite spots. Yolan's was always directly on her right, closest to her.

"Okay, now that we have taken out the trash let's talk business. Things are going well at the gallery. We have a shipment of 'new discoveries' from the motherland coming in for 'Punch' on the West Side. We are meeting with them next Monday. Joy and Rini, I need you both there and invisible. We haven't worked much with Punch so I need to make sure he's cool."

She watched as Joy scribbled down notes. She and Rini both nodded at her request; her face spread in a small, smug smile feeling a proud moment of the empire she and her ladies had built. She was glad everyone underestimated and counted them out because it made them all work that much harder. One thing Tayana made sure of was all of her ladies were educated and held degrees in their choice of study.

Tayana Bradley was cocoa butter brown with a perfect hourglass shape. She stood 5'3". Her oval shaped face and sparkling brown eyes made her stand out in crowds no matter how hard she tried to remain low-key. She looked flawless in whatever she chose to wear. She held a degree in art history and archeology as well as in business management. Besides English, she spoke six languages fluently: French, German, Spanish, Vietnamese, Arabic, and Italian.

Yolan looked over to make sure Tayana was finished before she started to give her report. "Well, business is going really well over at Royalty. Three new properties just came on the market you might want to look at before I post them in the open market. We cleared 6 million this month." Yolan passed her a copy of the listings.

Yolan was Tayana's best friend and second in command. There was not one memory she had that didn't contain Yolan. Their families were next-door neighbors and friends even before the girls were born. Yolan's mother still lived there, her father passed away a few years back from prostate cancer.

Yolan owned and ran a very lucrative real estate company, and she was in charge of the crew's imports. She was fluent in Mandarin, French, and Spanish. Yolan was curvy, short, and the color of bronze. She rocked her hair in a stylish short cut that complimented her baby doll face.

Just like Yolan, Shay and Monet looked over at her to make sure she was done before they began to give their report.

Above all, the crew knew to treat each and every one of their sisters with respect at all times. Petty shit like disrespect broke up crews and Tayana wasn't having any of that foolishness. She started out with a crew of twelve. When she found that some couldn't abide by her rules, she cut them loose with the threat of death if they ever spoke her name again.

"The boutique stays busy. We got some new pieces in from Milan and Morocco this month, we are selling out like crazy. The custom items from our new line are turning heads too. Our cleaning services have picked up two new clients. As it stands, we will be bringing in about seven million this month depending on how much cleaning we do." Monet passed the paperwork down the table to Tayana.

Shay had a business management degree and Monet had one in finance. They ran 'Lovelies' Boutique' together and laundered money for both foreign and domestic parties. Both spoke Chinese, Japanese, French, and Italian fluently. They both had an eye for business and fashion. Most of Tayana's clothes came from their boutique. They were also black belts in Jiu Jitsu, Karate, and Taekwondo; Monet had special talents with knives.

Shay stood 5' 9" with beautiful Hershey brown smooth skin. Her piercing eyes, full lips, and oval-shaped face gave her a naturally exotic look. Makeup was wasted on her unmarred skin; she was perfect without it.

Monet, who could have been and was often mistaken for Shay's sister, stood at 5'8". Ass and titties for days, it was her hazel brown eyes that kept the brothers sweating over her wherever she went.

Khyrs and Jaidyn were up next. "The salon is crazy busy! We are standing room only on most days. We have some VIP's coming in later this week that we need to do some things for, but we got it handled. Last month we made about 2.5 million overall." Jaidyn stood up and walked their paperwork to Tayana. They ran the hair salon 'Ghetto Star' and specialized in intelligence.

If there was anything Tayana needed information on, these were the two she went to. Khyrs' degree was in communications and Jaidyn's was in political science, but their love for all things hair and beauty had them living their dream running their own salon. Both were fluent in Spanish, Yoruba, and Creole French. Non-lethal weapons were their specialty so they were the ones normally called in for torture.

Khyrs was the color of peanut butter, 5'5", slanted eyes,

and long eyelashes. She was classically beautiful with a round face and thin lips. If not for her complexion, she could have been a white girl in another life.

Jaidyn was almond brown with high cheekbones, hooded sleepy eyes, and an infectious, girl next-door smile. She always rocked stilettos so no one really knew how tall she actually was.

Joy and Rini were up last. "The Firm is making money hand over fist. Looks like the public library will be signing a contract with us soon so we have slow and steady growth. Last month we took in 5 million." Joy passed their files to Rini who slid them across the table to Tayana.

Joy and Rini ran a security company and provided security all over the city. Joy held dual degrees in criminal law and criminal justice. Rini held hers in criminal justice. Both were lethal with or without weapons.

Joy was beautiful, but not in the soft and demure way. She worked out seven days a week and her body was muscular and tight but still very feminine. She was light skinned with a sprinkle of freckles on her nose. Her light brown hair was always styled in asymmetrical long braided designs.

Rini looked like everybody's baby sister. Full round face with dimples the color of cafe au lait. Curves for days, but she usually wore baggy, loose-fitting clothing to hide it. She rocked a short curly afro and gold hoops every day. Joy's languages of choice were Italian, French, Spanish and Vietnamese, Shay's were French, German, Italian and Nigerian.

"Very nice, ladies, keep up the good work. I appreciate all you do, never forget that. Without my ladies, I would have nothing. Now before we adjourn, is there any new business?"

Tayana tapped all the folders she'd been handed on the table to make a neat and even stack that she would review later. She trusted her crew but she kept an eye on things because the one thing she was not was a damn fool.

"We fired six people including two at the guard station. I will get some new guards out there from The Firm before nightfall. Both have worked for us for the last four years, loyal, good guys," Joy announced standing up from the table.

"Good looking out, Joy. If no one else here needs you for anything, you and Rini can go handle business. Bruise is still here and Mary Jane is strapped to my ankle like always."

All of her crew knew how to handle firearms with marksman-like precision. That was the one thing her father allowed her to learn, she took each lesson to heart and made sure her ladies did too.

No one had anything to add so Joy and Rini left the office.

"Anything else?" They all shook their heads in the negative.

"Okay, cool. Ladies, let's get it and remember, 'Quiet Moves are Successful Moves'."

Tayana walked briskly to her favorite Italian restaurant, checking her Shinola, mother of pearl faced watch for the twelfth time. She was almost late to meet with a buyer and tardiness was never acceptable, it showed you didn't respect either the client or their time and she refused to ever be that person.

Salvador stood as she approached. "Bellissima, as always," he murmured as he leaned close to kiss each of her cheeks in turn.

"Thanks, Sal, you look just as mouthwatering as always, too. Shall we order before or after we discuss business?" Tayana flirted, sitting across from him. He was one she had to ego stroke at all times.

"Why not during? I am famished after my travels abroad."

He opened his menu and immediately started discussing each dish that piqued his interest with her in detail.

Tayana opened her own menu and rolled her eyes before they landed directly on what she always ordered, fire-grilled, breadcrumb coated sea scallops and angel hair pasta. Now she had to act interested in all of his activities, including his sexual conquests, the man was an absolute bore and a boar!

"Excuse me? Ma'am, I was instructed to bring this to you immediately."

The hostess handed her a black business card with no words, just gold music notes and a saxophone.

Tayana immediately looked over at Bruise who was now seated two tables over from her own. His brow lifted in question and concern. Business meetings with the art buyers were never cause for alarm. He quickly closed his menu and began to scan the restaurant for potential threats.

"I'm sorry, who told you to give this to me? I mean, where did he go?" Tayana saw red. Someone was playing games, which was something she did not do, especially when it came to her business and her money.

"I'm so sorry, ma'am, he left just as I reached the table to deliver it." The hostess blushed, looking uncomfortable under Tayana's glare.

"Interesting. Do you happen to remember what he looks like, maybe?" Tayana asked, smiling sweetly over at Salvador who was watching the exchange with interest, stroking his salt and pepper beard covered chin.

"Let's see, he was tall with wavy hair, dressed and looked like a model. African American, his complexion was a few shades lighter than yours, with an amazing smile," the hostess answered, her eyes going all dreamy until she stopped describing the person behind the business card and looked nervously at the door as new customers walked in.

"Well, thank you. I think I know who that is." Tayana

turned the card over to check the other side before dropping it in her purse.

"So, does my beautiful Tayana have an admirer now?" Salvador teased as the waiter came to take their order.

"I highly doubt that, Salvador. Besides, I only have eyes for you," she murmured after giving her order, her mind was no longer on eating, however, as she was heated and seeing red.

After convincing Salvador he just couldn't live without two Renaissance original paintings she had recently purchased for his collection, she quick-stepped back to her car.

"Are you okay, Whisper?" Bruise asked, looking concerned as he opened her door.

"Yeah, B, I'm good. Just looks like I need to show someone I am not to be fucked with, that's all."

Tayana slid in the back of her car. Once the door was closed, she pulled the card back out of her clutch. She could understand the message Jazz was sending without a single word, *You ready for that talk?* Yeah, Jazz's ass had her all the way fucked up!

Two days later, Tayana stood in her gallery showroom directing her electrician on how the lighting should shine on the works of a local artist who was having his show at the gallery the next night.

The bell sounded as three men walked in. Two of them couldn't have looked more out of place if they tried. Their muscles bulged out of their ill-fitted silk suits looking like every 90's bouncer cliché come to life. Bodyguards. Dumb ones, but bodyguards, nonetheless. Jazz stepped out from behind them looking like he had just stepped off a GQ magazine shoot. His black Zegna suit riding his body perfectly.

Annoyed, Tayana continued to instruct the electrician on how to finish up before even acknowledging him.

About forty minutes later, she slowly walked over to Jazz. She was actually surprised he stayed in the gallery as long as he had. He was admiring a framed print by the African American artist WAK.

"Can I help you, sir?" she inquired politely, her smile was as venomous as the first time they met. She gazed past him out the gallery window, and clocked his real security detail in the parked car about three cars from the gallery entrance.

Jazz looked down at her, his eyes taking the time to admire her custom suit and her matching pumps. "Do you ignore all your customers like that or just me? Because if it's just me, let me assure you, Whisper, I am not the one you want to play games with," he warned, clearly annoyed he had been kept waiting.

Damn, the male ego ain't no joke! Tayana thought to herself before answering. "Oh, it's most definitely just you, Jazz, and believe me I am not the one you want to play games with either. Now for the second time since this conversation began, can I help you, *sir*? If you are here to waste my time, do us both a favor and don't. I do have a business to run." Tayana looked up at him, placing her hands on her hips waiting for his answer.

Jazz looked down at Tayana, his jaw jumped angrily, part of him wanted to shake her ass for disrespecting him, the other part of him wanted to grab her and kiss her like she obviously needed to be kissed.

"Well, Boss Lady, I realized I gave you my card but no number so I thought I should stop by and set an appointment for our talk." Jazz strolled to the next painting, whistling through his teeth.

"Or, to cut through all the bullshit, you are here to prove you have eyes on me and know how to find me anytime you want to, right?" she snapped moving along with him as he strolled and whistled. He could tell she was trying not to show it, but he was really pissing her off, good.

He looked at her in mock surprise. "Such harsh language, Boss Lady. Why would I do something like that? I am just a businessman trying to set up a business meeting with a businesswoman. What is the harm in that? I like this one, how much is it?" He pointed to the painting he was standing in front of.

"If you have to ask, then you can't afford it. Now about this *talk* you are so anxious to have with me. Why? What have I done to pique your interest this much, Jazz?" Tayana asked.

He could tell she was still fighting to maintain control, his mouth practically watered at the thought of the fun he was going to have taking it away from her. "As I said the night we met, I know everyone in Houston, but I don't know you. I aim to rectify that oversight." Jazz pulled out his checkbook and looked over at her expectantly.

She looked from him to his checkbook thoughtfully. "Hmm, interesting. I like not being known, Jazz, and don't see a reason to change what works. Now, then, our *talk* is over and that painting is $15,000. Once you've made your purchase, Joy and Rini will arrange for the delivery." Tayana led him to the desk where her security now sat. "Goodbye, Jazz, and thank you for your business."

Tayana turned to walk away from him without even so much as a backward glance but he wasn't having it. He stepped in front of her preventing her from exiting. "On the contrary, Boss Lady, our 'talk' has only just begun." From the lethal glare she gave him he could tell she wasn't used to people stopping her from doing what she wanted to do, but she would soon find out, when it came to him, he called the shots in all things and he was not one for disrespect of any kind.

"By the way, did you get my flowers, Tayana?" he asked, without even looking up to see her reaction as he wrote out his check. He knew if anything would rattle her cage, the admission he was responsible for the flowers would.

Tayana's eyes narrowed as she looked up at him, "I should have known," she began, shaking her head with an incredulous smile. "Jazz, let me give you some friendly advice. I don't like games, power plays, or cocky, small-minded men who feel I am a toy to wind up at their whim. Now, for the last time, before I lose my patience and allow Joy to put you out of your misery, what do you want with me or from me?" she asked, barely above a deadly whisper.

He turned and took her lightly by the upper arm and walked her over to the security desk to Joy and Rini. "Like I have said three times now, I want to talk to you. What I want is for us to arrange a meeting or do we continue this little dance we're doing? Because I guarantee you, you will get tired of the steps way before I do," he stated, while handing Joy, who was now glaring at him, the check he wrote. His demeanor was unbothered and light.

Tayana looked up at Jazz's handsome face and shook her head trying her best to check her temper. "You're bold, I will give you that. I can't tell if that's just who you are or if you underestimate who I am. Either way, it's not too smart on your part. Rini, arrange a meeting and let me know where and when. Joy, put that gun away... for now," Tayana ordered before moving out of his grasp.

She tried to maintain the mask of indifference as her hormones began to let her know how attracted she was to this man. The sound of Joy's gun uncocking echoed through the empty showroom. "Now that you have your meeting, is it safe to say I am free to leave?" Tayana asked biting the inside of her cheek, her face feeling hot and flushed. The words that just left her lips felt foreign and uncomfortable to her, she was not the kind of women who asked for permission to do anything and yet she was basically asking him if she could leave her own damn place of business! What the fuck was that about?

"You're the boss, right?" he quipped with a smirk and lifted eyebrow in her direction. "Until next time, Boss Lady, goodnight," he said bringing her hand to his lips letting the tip of his tongue taste her skin.

The feeling of want that ricocheted through her was instantaneous. "Good night, Jazz," she managed to say, before turning quickly and rushing out of the gallery to her car out back. Tayana took a few moments to regain her composure as she slipped into the back seat of her car. She had known Jazz would pop up somewhere since he gave her that card and it would be in her space when it happened, somewhere she was comfortable. No matter how strong her reaction to him was, he was still playing games, stupid ass games! What the hell was the fucking point?

"Hold tight for a minute, B. This fool, Jazz, thinks I'm to be taken lightly. He brought two muscle heads in with him and Rini and Joy are still inside," Tayana said and pulled Mary Jane out of her holster and slipped off her heels.

She and Bruise crept to the side entrance and the back way to the gallery. She heard Jazz trying to engage Joy and Rini in small talk while the two muscle heads stood behind her ladies – a little too close behind her ladies – they had moved closer than they were a few minutes before.

They were shifting their weight nervously from one foot to the other, looking over their shoulders at the car outside giving up the security details' location. *Where the fuck did he find these idiots?* she thought to herself. Instead of bothering her, his ass needed to be addressing the chinks in the armor of his crew!

"So, how long have you known, Whisper?" Jazz asked, while filling out the delivery slip. Nothing but silence came from Joy and Rini.

"That long, huh? That's what's up," he answered while smiling, actually looking like he was having the time of his life. He handed the slip over to Rini who silently passed him a card with what Tayana knew was the location and time for their agreed upon meeting.

"Damn man, can we leave now? All these bitches and their stank ass attitudes have worked my last nerve!" Muscle Head Number One snapped at Jazz, who quietly and slowly put his checkbook back into his jacket pocket.

"Ay, Joy, can you box?" Jazz asked leaning on the desk, ignoring his security altogether.

Tayana knew Joy was heated, calling her a bitch was a death wish but, true to form, she didn't answer Jazz. It didn't matter which one of her ladies it was, he would have gotten the same response. Until Tayana said an outsider was cool, the ladies maintained their silence, even then they didn't say much.

"What about you? Rini, right? Can you fight? You know, throw down?"

Rini stood ramrod straight and silent, staring at something beyond Jazz's head.

"Hmm, well let me ask you this, what would you do if Boss Lady was here and that fool said what he just said?" Jazz asked, still leaning on the counter looking from woman to woman.

Still neither Joy nor Rini answered.

"Interesting," was all Jazz said, as he walked over to the door and the muscle heads. With a backward glance to Joy and Rini, he backhanded the one with the mouth. "Apologize," he growled, straightening his jacket.

The security guard covered his bleeding mouth in surprise. "What the fuck, man?" he shouted, looking angrily at Jazz.

Jazz gave him a deadly look. "I said apologize for disrespecting the ladies." His voice was low and dipped in venom. "The fact I had to tell you twice has me feeling some type of way," Jazz informed him, getting up in the bodyguard's personal space. "Now apologize and open the fucking door. Remember who the fuck you work for," Jazz growled, looking angry for the first time since he walked into the gallery.

The bodyguard forced out a quick apology to Joy and Rini before holding the door open for Jazz with his free hand.

"Tell Boss Lady, I look forward to our talk." Jazz moved to walk out of the door and saw the drops of blood on the floor from the bodyguard's mouth. "Clean that shit up," he barked at his other security guard before moving around the blood and out of the door. The second security guard pulled out his handkerchief and quickly mopped the blood off the floor before he left, too.

"Boss Lady?" Joy turned, her eyes met Tayana's through the black curtain that hid the side entrance.

Tayana walked into the room, tucking Mary Jane into the small of her back.

"Enjoy the show?" Joy asked, now fighting back her smile.

"But of course. Not that I'm surprised, but good job keeping it together, ladies. Although, the next time he acts out that scene, he should get better actors, don't you think?" Tayana walked over to the gallery entrance and locked the double doors and dimmed the lights.

Chapter 3

Jazz sat in his office turning the card Rini gave him over and over in his hands. Again he had to admit he was more than a little impressed with Tayana and her crew. The fact neither Rini nor Joy even blinked in his direction because Tayana didn't react to the information about the flowers still had him tripping, it cemented what he'd heard, her crew operated with class and she was in complete control.

Tayana. Everything about her intrigued him. He had never come across a woman like her before in his life, and the more he knew, the more he had to know.

In his mind's eye he kept fantasizing about her completely under his control as she moaned his name in her screams of passion. He knew it would be a reality sooner rather than later because what Jazz Jones wants, Jazz Jones always gets.

"Why does he still have a fucking pulse, is what I want to know!" Shay sat back hard in her chair angrily.

Her crew was waiting in her office when she arrived home that evening, just as she requested. Joy paced back and forth in the back of the room, taking calming breaths.

Tayana's eyebrow arched in Shay's direction. None of her ladies questioned her decisions, they knew she had a reason for everything she did and would fill them in when the time was right.

"I didn't mean any disrespect, Whisper, but he came here! Here to your house, uninvited, leaving threats and shit!" Shay quickly reasoned. "For that alone he deserves a beat down at the very least. I need the practice, anyway. Let me and Mo put something on him," Shay offered with an evil grin. Monet was by far the deadliest of their crew, when she put in work it was never pretty.

"Shay, I understand why you are upset. I understand why all of you are upset but know this, everything I do and every move I make is for us. To answer your question and maybe all of your questions, he has a pulse because of who he is, period. Jazz Jones is the King of Houston and he knows if we touch him we're done. That being said, the fact we rose up so swiftly and undetected by all the major players, especially Mr. Jones, bothers him. So now he wants to know more about us, how we did it, how we operate and most of all if we are a threat to him and his business. Until I meet with him, to sate his curiosity, he will be coming at us from all directions looking for weakness. His boys will be coming too, so get ready and pay attention. Now, more than ever, we have to stand united, ladies. If there is any ill will or anything less than productive thoughts rolling around in those pretty heads of yours, let's address them now. We won't have another chance before he comes at us."

All her ladies looked around at each other before all shaking their heads in the negative.

"We are with you, Tay, one-hundred percent, and we're

ready. If Jazz and his crew want to start some shit, we're ready for them." Yolan reached over and squeezed Tayana's hand.

All the ladies nodded in agreement; all verbalized their readiness to stand with the rest of the crew.

"All right then. Khyrs and Jaidyn, I need to know more than the basics on Jazz. I want to know his preschool teacher's name, ya feel me? Shay and Monet, I have a special project for you and the boutique. I need you to order the best of the best in men's clothing and promote the hell out of it. I know of one of his weaknesses so we might as well exploit it."

"I know of another one," Joy announced, finally settling in a seat. Everyone turned to look at her.

Tayana looked up at Joy in surprise. "You do? How the hell did I miss it?"

Joy shrugged. "Because it's you, Boss Lady." A smile tugged at her lips.

Tayana looked over at Yolan who was nodding enthusiastically. "Yep, I clocked that too, Joy. That night in the VIP he was sending you all kinds of signals with those light eyes, Tay!"

Tayana felt a flutter in her stomach at the thought of Jazz's light eyes and handsome ass smile but pushed it down deep in the recesses of her mind. "Fuck that! Jazz is just trying to come at me like a suitor to knock me off balance, it's all part of his game," she argued, refusing to even entertain something so off base. Her and Jazz Jones would never work even if he was serious, she liked being the boss in all things and she could tell he did, too, they would do nothing but butt heads constantly.

"Whisper, all of us here at this table know and love you and one of your most famous, and maybe only fault, is ignoring what you don't want to acknowledge or see. He risked everything when he admitted to those flowers. Those two buffoons that came in with him weren't even packing. Even if he didn't admit it, he knew I had my gun cocked and ready by the time you brought him to the desk. He wants you, Whisper. Something about you has got to him." Joy smiled over at her again.

"Joy, he knows we can't touch him without bringing unwanted attention to ourselves. Don't lose focus, ladies. If there is nothing else, consider this subject closed. Ms. Lanie is ready to serve dinner for those who want to stay," Tayana snapped and stood exiting her office, her ladies remained seated.

"Y'all already know what's up, we gotta keep an even closer eye on her now. The last pretty motherfucker almost got our girl killed and we ain't having it. Ay, Khyrs, do me a favor add past relationships to that list and if anything comes back funny, you know what to do. Joy, you good?" Yolan stood and moved to the door, all the ladies followed.

"Yeah, I'm good but I promise you, this one? If he's foul, I'm disappearing his ass! Now let's go see what Ms. Lanie made because my stomach is screaming at my back, it's so empty."

Tayana stood in front of her mirror and contemplated what to wear to her meeting with Jazz and it pissed her off! This was not her; she picked her outfits based on what she was attempting to communicate at that time, and every time she thought of this meeting she had nothing. More than half of her walk-in closet was tossed in a discarded pile on her bed.

"Fuck this." She crossed the room and sent a text to Shay and Monet.

Putting on a pair of shorts and a button-down shirt, she flopped down in front of her lighted mirror and brushed her hair.

Twenty minutes later, Shay and Monet knocked at the

door and walked into her room carrying garment bags followed by Khyrs and Jaidyn. "We figured if wardrobe choices were giving you such a fit, then hair and makeup must be too," Shay said, unzipping the garment bags.

"Good looking out but if the four of you are here who is running the businesses?" Tayana asked, looking at them through her mirror.

"Yolan said that would be the first thing you said, so now I owe that heffa lunch, damn! To answer your question, Yolan and Rini are at the Salon, and Joy and Cisco from The Firm are at the boutique. It's a Tuesday, so business is steady but not crazy so we can be spared to help you. Cool?" Shay asked and pulled out the first of the six outfits she brought for Tayana.

Two hours later Tayana arrived at Spindletop for her meeting with Jazz. Her ladies had hooked her up! Her plum handkerchief hemmed dress played off her skin tone perfectly. Her Jimmy Choo's were a shade darker on purpose. Shoes this pretty needed to be highlighted and a clothes whore like Jazz was sure to notice. Her long, dark brown hair was styled in a slipknot at the base of her neck and the ends of her hair tickled her bare back. Her makeup was fierce but appeared effortless, bringing special attention to her eyes and lips. They even insisted she wear her favorite perfume from Pakistan, *BVLGARI Le Gemme*. Just in case Joy was right, they made sure if he liked her now then he would love her enough to reveal his true intentions by the end of the night.

After passing her pashmina to the maître d', Tayana followed him to her private table and waited. She ordered ginger ale in a champagne flute but had the waiter bring a bottle of Ace of Spades champagne on ice to the table as well. Tonight, Joy and Rini were behind the scenes. Her ladies, sans

Yolan, were scattered throughout the restaurant, blending in. Yolan was on standby in case things got ugly.

"Miss Bradley, your guest has arrived," her waiter announced and showed Jazz to his seat. He popped the champagne and poured a glass, setting it in front of Jazz with a flourish.

"Your idea?" Jazz asked as he took a seat and picked up the champagne flute.

Tayana took a sip of her own drink while noting his detail was being escorted to a table next to Monet's. For a brief moment, she watched as they were seated, fearing they knew Monet was hers, but when one of his boys did a double take to stare a little longer, she knew his interest in Monet had nothing to do with business.

She shifted her gaze two tables over to an elderly couple sitting on the same side of the table and smiled.

"So, Boss Lady does have a heart." Jazz sat back, following her gaze.

Tayana dropped her smile and looked over at him, slowly sipping her ginger ale. "I'm sorry?" she asked him to clarify to buy herself some time, he was watching her every move and she didn't like her reaction to it, he had only been there about ten minutes and his eyes on her already had her hormones singing. Besides, she couldn't show animosity, at least not yet.

"I was simply stating it was nice to see some genuine emotion from you. Now, again, was the champagne your idea?" he asked while taking a sip, narrowing his eyes in annoyance at her.

"Well, I saw how you and your boys celebrated in the VIP so I thought it was a nice goodwill gesture," she lied. She knew he hated it, he wasn't the Ace of Spades type. She knew so much more about him than before all thanks to Khyrs and Jaidyn. They were very thorough, especially about his love life. It was an interesting read indeed.

"Not the case? Please allow me to rectify that," she stated, when he winced from the taste and shook his head. Tayana signaled for their waiter who was standing by.

"Yes, ma'am?" The waiter leaned in slightly.

"The gentleman doesn't care for the champagne, could you bring a cognac instead? *Tesseron Extreme* if you have it," she requested, smiling knowingly over at Jazz. She had the cognac ordered the entire time.

"Of course. My apologies for the inconvenience." Their waiter cleared away the champagne and the flute Jazz had been drinking from.

Jazz stared across the table at her before nodding slowly. "Impressive, I like how you move, Boss Lady. Even when you are no longer in control of the situation, you are always thinking and planning," he said, saluting her with the glass of dark liquor that was just set in front of him.

Tayana fought the urge to glare at him, his statement of her no longer being in control wasn't sitting right with her. What the hell? "Now that we have the drink situation under control, shall we proceed? I believe you have gone to great lengths to meet with me."

Tayana sat back taking another leisurely drink from her flute. His expertly tailored gray suit brought out hues of gray-green in his eyes. His fade was freshly cut, mustache and goatee were neatly trimmed as well. Why did he have to be so damn good looking? Fuck, her growing attraction to him was not okay! Under normal circumstances she might even welcome his advances but given their present circumstances, not so much; it was downright unnerving.

"Indeed I have. I must say, Whisper, you and your operations are impressive. A very well-oiled machine," he stated with a calculated look cast in her direction.

Tayana sighed, placing her flute back on the table in front of her. "You know, Jazz, while most people in our line of work enjoy a little ego stroking, I do not. I know how successful I am. I don't need Jazz Jones of Houston to tell me what I already know. Now, shall we move on to the next topic?"

His deadly gaze had made a return, his light-colored eyes darkened in annoyance, she could tell her dismissive attitude was getting to him. "What is our next topic, Boss Lady?" he asked dangerously low, his jaw working as he ground his teeth. "Because you and that swift tongue of yours are making me feel some type of way and you are dangerously close to getting a reaction you are not ready for just yet," he warned, taking another healthy swallow of his drink.

"Interesting. Nonetheless, the only subject I want to discuss is what is it you want, Jazz. I have had enough of this game of chase we seem to be playing." Tayana crossed her legs, staring across the table at him.

Jazz picked up his cognac and emptied the glass, his eyes darkened and flashed as he looked at her. "You. That's what I want, Tayana," he stated, looking serious and determined as he signaled the waiter for a refill while still staring at her.

"How unfortunate," she stated and picked a wayward thread from the hem of her dress, shaking her head.

"What is?" he asked, taking a sip from his water glass while he waited on his drink.

Tayana could tell he was beginning to have a hard time controlling his frustration and a small, knowing smile spread across her beautiful face. Even though he kept his calm and laid-back facade, his movements weren't as smooth and deliberate as he prided himself on and she picked up on it. The look on his face showed he wanted to say more to reprimand her behavior but, instead he thanked the waiter for his drink refill and took a big swallow of it.

"What is unfortunate is the fact you are still insistent on playing games with me, Jazz. I had honestly hoped by my agreeing to this meeting we could move past this part of our, what's a good word… encounters with one another." Her venomous smile had returned.

It actually made him feel better that it appeared she wanted this meeting over with more than ever now. Jazz, it seemed her own frustration level was reaching its peak. Little did she know his frustration was for a very different reason than business, the strong response from being this close to her was taking him through some serious changes.

His eyes narrowed. "Have you always been like this, Tayana?" he asked, refusing to call her 'Whisper'. The kind of relationship he aimed to have with her was too intimate for her street name. He swirled the ice and dark liquid around in his glass thinking about her giving in to him completely.

Signaling the waiter to refill her ginger ale, Tayana narrowed her own eyes, looking both impatient and annoyed. "You tell me, Jazz. I'm sure you already know."

Jazz's need to snatch her out of her chair, and warm her ass with his hand was at an all-time high, but instead he leaned in meeting her eyes. "All right, Boss Lady. I tell you what, I will show you mine if you show me yours." His eyes drifted down to her cleavage for a brief moment, and he licked his lips. Fuck, he wanted her.

Tayana smiled her venomous smile again. "Finally we're getting somewhere, shall we begin?" she asked sitting back, she repositioned herself and crossed her legs towards Jazz, instead of away from him, giving a glimpse of her upper thigh.

Jazz downed his cognac and cleared his throat. "Tayana 'Whisper' Bradley. Youngest and only daughter of Kingpin, Jason 'Heavy' Bradley, of Wichita Falls, TX and Essie Bradley. You graduated from Hirschi High School in 2005 with honors and voted most likely to succeed. You've earned three degrees including a Masters in art and archaeology. Your parents are both deceased. Siblings, you have two brothers: Calvin Bradley currently residing in Japan, and Melvin 'Man' Bradley in Europe. Your name appears on several properties and businesses in the greater Houston area, all legitimate and all thriving quite well but only one has you listed as sole owner; your gallery 'Essie's' is named for your deceased mother. The only love interest I was able to dig up was a cat named Theo Walton from the eighth grade and, trust me, I looked far and wide for the man who broke your heart. I figured he has to be the reason you throw off that unapproachable, don't touch me vibe," he stated, looking over at her smugly while sitting back in his own chair.

Tayana listened with an amused look on her face. "Thorough, very thorough, and as per usual it's assumed there has to be a man who made me the way I am, because what? A woman can't be driven and focused on handling her business without some life-altering event caused by a man happening in her life? How unoriginal that you took the easy way out." She brought her glass to her lips shaking her head with feigned disappointment.

Jazz looked over at her, ignoring her smart-ass comment and licked his lips like he was ready to taste something he'd been waiting a long time for. "Your turn." He felt his eyes getting heavy from the cognac and switched to water, he needed to hear all she had to say so he could figure out his next plan of attack.

"Jazz Jones, yes that's right your mother named you Jazz after an old love named Jazzcat she had a summer romance with, but never saw again, and never got over him. You are an only child. You were born in Longview but you moved to Houston at the age of two. You dropped out of school in the 7th grade and became a corner boy. You quickly rose through the ranks and by the time you were old enough to vote you were second in command to Steven 'Slick' Sims. Your mother, a recovering drug addict, is now a born again Christian and plays the piano at Silver Star Baptist Church in Columbus Georgia. You speak to her once a week, you pray together. You also send her two dozen peach roses every other week, which makes it all the more interesting you sent me the same color. The last time they were delivered to her was yesterday, by the way. No love interests to speak of as you don't really trust women other than your mother after your fiancée, Patricia Thomas, messed around and got pregnant by Slick. Neither, I might add, are still with us. I think that's enough, for now, don't you?" Tayana asked.

His jaw clenched in anger, his eyes darkened as he took in this beautiful woman in front of him watching her quietly. Getting her where he wanted her was not going to be easy, she had been in control most of her life, but she would be worth the effort because he wanted her more now than he did before.

She took a deep breath and continued, "Now, Jazz, as you can see your reach is long, but I can guarantee mine is longer. That being said, I, nor my ladies, have any intention or interest in impeding your business in any way, shape, or form. As I told you before, I like being unnoticed, in fact, I welcome it. My crew and I are content where we are and have no ideas of grandeur. Raz and Jammy just happened to be common enemies between us, no ill will or disrespect intended. Since you now know my true intentions I hope this concludes our *talk* and I can go back to being unnoticed." Tayana took a drink from her water glass and waited.

Jazz took in a deep drink of water and sighed. "That would be all well and good if not for one thing, Tayana," he said, licking his lips as he looked over at her, his gaze moving slowly from head to toe. By the way her nipples hardened beneath her dress and her breathing had become a little labored he could tell he was getting to her even though she was still trying to play it cool.

Tayana squirmed in her chair, signaled the waiter for their check, and laid down her platinum American Express card. "And what might that be, Jazz?" she asked, after she finished her water.

He noticed her pulse dancing rapidly on the side of her beautiful neck and longed to kiss her there, the smell of her perfume was captivating. Jazz stopped the waiter and pulled out his own card and slid Tayana's across the table to her.

"I did notice you." Jazz's eyes met hers across the table. "And, once more, I want you, and I am used to getting what I want," he said leaning forward, looking deep into her eyes, throwing her all kinds of signals, making his intentions very clear.

Tayana tucked her card back in her purse and stood up from the table, her pashmina was draped over her shoulders as she tucked her clutch under her arm before walking over to Jazz. Smiling down at him, she ran her hand softly down the side of his handsome face. "And as I said before, that's unfortunate. Goodnight, Jazz," she whispered against his ear, she felt him swallow hard in response while looking straight ahead.

Jazz grabbed her hand and brought it to his lips kissing her on the pulse point of her wrist before pulling her down into his lap before she could even react. He ran his middle finger down her back causing her to arch it, when she did he grabbed her by the back of the head forcing his tongue deep into her mouth, Tayana moaned involuntarily as their lips met in a curious yet passionate kiss and just when she was reveling in the wonderful taste of him, he pulled his lips away from hers and moved her off of his lap, standing with his hands on her waist to steady her.

"Believe me, Tayana, the only thing that is unfortunate when it comes to me and you is how hell bent and determined you are to fight the inevitable. That rush of emotion you're feeling right now, get used to it because neither it nor me are going anywhere anytime soon," Jazz told her, running his thumb softly across her bottom lip. "Have a good night, Tayana, and dream of me because I will most definitely be dreaming of you." He readjusted her pashmina on her shoulders before letting her go and reclaiming his seat.

Tayana took a step backwards before turning and crossing the restaurant on shaking legs, his touch and kiss had ignited something in her she thought she had long forgotten was even there. She felt Jazz's heated gaze on her as she left. Climbing into the back of her car, she let out a slow breath and reached up to push a hair out of her face, she noticed her hand smelled like his cologne, which made her cross her legs tightly from the fire building there.

She replayed every detail of their conversation to look for deception but the only thing she could remember clearly was those sexy ass eyes of his and that he'd told her he wanted her.

"Shit!" was all Tayana said, before closing her eyes trying to erase the look on his face as she reached out to touch him and his lips grazed the inside of her wrist. No matter how hard she tried to fight it, the truth remained, she wanted him, too.

―――――――――

Jazz sat at the table and waited for the waiter to bring back his card, biting the inside of his cheek, while his dick pressed painfully against his slacks, fully erect in response to his first taste of Tayana.

He knew now the typical hearts and flowers approach wasn't going to work to get her to let her guard down and yield to him. A woman like Tayana was unimpressed with the ordinary and would most likely ignore those types of gestures altogether. He needed something huge to pull her in and gain her trust if he was ever going to get her to submit to his will. What he had in mind would take some time, but good things always come to those who wait, and he had the patience of Job when he was focused on the end result.

Chapter 4

Two Weeks Later

"There she is," Jazz said, strolling confidently over to Tayana with his hands behind his back as he entered the gallery with a smile on his face. "The woman who continuously manages to take my breath away." His eyes took inventory of her body in a leisurely fashion, she looked sexy as hell in everything she wore even when she wasn't trying to, times like now.

"If it isn't Mr. Jones. I have to admit I am more than a bit surprised to see you here at my gallery, uninvited, again," Tayana said quickly looking up from the clipboard she was writing on when she heard his voice. He saw the smallest hint of a blush in her cheeks. She now had a starring role in his dreams and fantasies alike since they had drinks together.

"I happen to love being in the presence of beautiful things. Surely I don't need an invitation for that, do I? And as far as you being surprised, I don't see why. You and I still have some unfinished business, Tayana," he said, handing her the bouquet of dark purple roses and violets from behind his back.

Her eyes lit up in surprise, a genuine smile on her face as she accepted them.

"These are beautiful, Jazz, thank you," she said, holding the flowers up to her nose, inhaling deeply, and smiling even bigger. "I can honestly say I'm touched."

"Beautiful flowers for a breathtakingly beautiful woman," he said, moving in closer to her. Her perfume, shit who was he kidding? Her very presence was wreaking havoc on his senses.

"Again I have to say thank you," she replied, handing off the flowers to a young woman who seemed to have appeared beside them out of nowhere. "Put these in water for me, please," Tayana ordered and stood silently as they both watched the woman disappear down a long hallway Jazz suspected led to Tayana's office.

"As lovely as the flowers are it still doesn't keep me from wondering exactly why you're here," Tayana stated looking up at him after a door opened and closed at the other end of the hallway.

"I came for this." Jazz stepped even closer invading Tayana's personal space, pulled her body against his and leaned down, pressing his lips against hers and pushing his tongue inside of her mouth. Since the restaurant he had not been able to get the taste of her, the smell of her, or the feel of her out of his system. He had tried to play it cool, be patient even. But her constantly side stepping his invitations to go out and the want he had for her, which was now deeply rooted inside of him, forced his hand. He decided it was past time to take action so she had no doubt of his intentions. "Well, that and to tell you to clear your schedule on Saturday," he said, when he finally pulled his lips from hers, tasting her again had his ravenous appetite causing his dick to twitch behind his zipper.

"Again, I have to say how unfortunate." Tayana sighed and took a step backwards to put some distance between them, despite her words her eyes were dilated with desire, her chest rose and fell rapidly. "Because unless your sole purpose was to deliver those beautiful flowers and or to purchase other original pieces of art, you wasted a trip."

Jazz chuckled as he pulled her close again. He was sure she wasn't one for public displays of affection, or anything that would draw attention to her private life, which was why he kept doing it. How badly he wanted her only enhanced his desire to keep touching her. "You say that like I gave you a choice or something," Jazz replied, his light eyes staring down at her.

"Whether you gave me a choice or not doesn't really matter, Jazz. I cannot and will not cancel the plans I have for Saturday," she stated moving out of his grasp for the second time, glancing around the empty show room.

"Which are?" he pressed trying to keep his temper in check, sooner or later she would have to learn telling him 'no' was not an option for her.

"I'm sorry?" she asked with a frown and shrug.

It was another thorn in her side, she had a problem being questioned about anything. Yeah, he had her entirely out of her comfort zone, but he didn't care. He wanted her with him and he was tired of waiting.

"What are your plans for Saturday, Tayana?" he ground out menacingly. "Because as I just told you I ain't asking."

"Look, I can certainly understand your frustration, Jazz. Especially considering the fact things are not going your way at the moment, but like I told you, I have plans, unbreakable plans." Tayana smirked, putting her hands on her hips, glaring up at him. "Not that I owe you an explanation but, to sate your curiosity, I will be out of town Saturday and I will reach out as I see fit when I get back," she offered with her venomous smile still looking up at him and shifting all of her weight to one side, a look of annoyance on her face.

"No need, Tayana," he said leaning down kissing her lips softly. "I know where you are and how to find you," he told her with a sinister grin and a wink before he turned and walked towards the gallery doors to leave while whistling a happy tune. She could run all she wanted, but it was time she learned how powerful he really was, and there was nowhere on God's green earth she could hide, even if she tried.

Tayana watched from her lounge chair next to the pool, as Monet snuck up on Yolan from the beach with a water gun full of cold water. Yolan was face down, eyes closed a few chairs down from her. It was almost like watching real life in slow motion as the cold water reached Yolan's back and she jumped up off the lounger.

"Mo! Imma kick your ass! You got my hair wet, heffa!" Yolan was on her feet and after Monet in one fluid motion.

She and the ladies were on their annual vacation weekend. It was a long weekend actually because they always left on Thursday and returned late the following Monday.

They worked hard and Tayana made sure she and her ladies had some down time. This year they had chosen a private beach house in the Bahamas, this was day two of their fun in the sun.

Tayana laughed as she watched them chase each other down the beach, damn she loved her ladies and best friends, they really were her everything.

Joy and Rini were playing volleyball nearby with their neighbors a few houses down the beach. Khyrs and Shay had just returned from shopping and were now napping in the air-conditioned house. Jaidyn was by herself on the beach under an umbrella reading a book by Sonovia Alexander. She was a die-hard fan of street lit.

Bruise and The Firm crew were holding down things at home until they got back. She had all of their businesses under constant surveillance on her laptop in case someone wanted to get stupid. These were the plans she refused to break and while she knew it pissed Jazz off she couldn't care less because her time with them was important.

Tayana lay back and closed her eyes, sighing contently. Life was good and getting better even with Jazz popping up whenever he wanted, knocking her off balance like he did at the gallery the other day. Her lips still tingled when she replayed how good his lips felt pressed against hers, how safe and right she felt when he held her close. She would never admit it to her crew, no matter how much they teased her about it, but she really liked Jazz's demanding, pushy demeanor and she was beginning to feel something genuine for him. Honestly, after all she had been through in the past, it scared the hell out of her. Unable to push him and his sexy ass light-colored eyes out of her head, she still allowed the sound of her friends' laughter and the call of the ocean to lull her to sleep.

One minute she was in a dreamless sleep, the next minute the sound of guns cocking in rapid succession snatched her back from her impromptu nap and into reality. Her eyes were barely open before she had Mary Jane cocked and ready to sing having no idea what was going on.

Tayana focused on the scene in front of her and blinked about a hundred times before pulling off her sunglasses. Jazz was standing on the beach in the middle of her ladies with his hands up. He was barefoot in a pair of Gucci shorts and no shirt.

I know you're fucking lying, she thought to herself as she

slowly walked down to the sand and stood in front of him, aiming Mary Jane at his forehead. "Explain."

"Boss Lady, I swear I didn't know this was you. I am out here with my mom and some of the ladies from her church. We are in the house over there." He pointed to the biggest house on their stretch of the beach. "My mom and them just got back from shopping and decided to watch a movie before dinner. I was restless and decided to take a walk. It wasn't until I walked up to see if I could join the game that I realized it was you and your crew," he explained looking surprised and nervous as hell on the surface, but she saw the small light of mischief dancing in his light eyes as he winked at her. She shouldn't even be surprised, he did tell her he knew where to find her when he left the gallery the other day, and it looked like he wasn't playing.

Tayana noticed Jazz's light skin was sun-kissed and a few shades darker, he even had tan lines on his shoulders from wearing tank-tops and it made her wonder how long he'd been in the Bahamas before coming over to their side of the beach. Because if she had to guess it seemed like his ass came here straight from the gallery, sneaky bastard! .

"Unbelievable," Tayana murmured as she uncocked Mary Jane and turned to return to her lounge chair, even as sexy as a shirtless Jazz was, she needed to get her hormones in check and think this situation through clearly. If he was able find her this easily she had to wonder who else could.

"Ladies, let him live for now," Tayana called over her shoulder as she went. She hated to admit it but she was flattered he would go to such lengths. No other man had ever put in that kind of effort, but he had exposed some kinks in the armor of her operation and that was not something she could afford to take lightly.

One by one her ladies uncocked their guns but stayed close to Jazz.

"Fuck!" Tayana swore under her breath, as she looked up and noticed the neighbors, who Joy and Rini were playing volleyball with, were peeping the whole scene with rabid interest. She also spotted a cellphone obviously recording.

"Joy?" Tayana called softly. Joy followed her line of vision and motioned for Yolan to follow her. They stowed their guns quickly and volunteered to walk their neighbors home.

The neighbors all cast one last curious glance over their shoulders towards Jazz, and the remaining ladies surrounding him, before they disappeared down the beach being escorted by Joy and Yolan.

Jazz watched the exchange and their retreating backs before turning back to Tayana. He took a tentative step in her direction. "Is this cool or will they shoot me in the back?"

Tayana settled back in her lounge chair, put Mary Jane away, and slid her sunglasses back on. "Not unless I tell them to," she answered indifferently.

Jazz walked slowly towards her with the sun at his back and his muscular frame on display making her damn near salivate, damn. What the fuck was up with her and this annoying ass man? He was everything she, for damn sure, didn't need in her life now, or ever. Why couldn't he just leave her alone? Just look at the havoc he caused in the five minutes he'd been there.

He stood in front of her briefly, hands on his hips before sitting down on the lounger next to her. He was sitting sideways facing her, feet planted on the ground, his hands clasped in between his knees.

"Damn, even on vacation you're still on high alert. Do you ever relax, Boss Lady?" he asked, shaking his head looking down at her.

"I *was* relaxed until you showed up," Tayana snapped, and flipped the pages of her trash mag refusing to look at him.

"Now tell me, how the hell did you find me, Jazz?" she asked still flipping pages.

"I am a man of many talents and resources, Tayana, and I will say finding you would have been impossible for an average man, you are quite good at moving under the radar but not so good that you could ever manage to get from under me," he quipped, plucking her magazine from her hands. His remark and him taking her magazine had her turning her head in an instant to glare in his direction, before taking a sip from her bottle of water she had picked up from beside the lounge.

"Is there something particular you meant with that last remark, Mr. Jones?" she asked still giving him the evil eye.

"Oh, you know exactly what I meant, Tayana, keep playing clueless if you want, you'll find out my full meaning even sooner than you think," he warned reaching out and using his finger to remove a droplet of water from her bottom lip. Tayana tried to ignore the tingle that moved through as that small bit of contact from him sent a signal of desire right between her legs.

"Now, shall we pick up where we left off at the gallery?" he asked her, dropping her magazine on top of the bag next to her chair. Figuring out where she was going hadn't been an easy feat but in the end he had gotten it done and it was well worth the effort, seeing Tayana in a bathing suit had him about to lose control.

He had been fighting the urge to allow his eyes to bug out of his head since he saw her, Tayana was wearing a bronze-colored bikini that, at first glance, against her cocoa butter skin looked like she was nude.

For someone who said she liked being unnoticed, she most definitely picked the wrong clothes to do it in. He loved her fashion sense and taste in clothes but at the moment his mind was racing, wondering if she looked as good, as he thought she did, out of them. He actually had to chuckle at his wayward thoughts, especially since less than five minutes ago he unexpectedly had seven guns aimed at him, eight if he counted Tayana's and all he could think about was what she looked like naked, yeah it was official, this woman was driving him straight out of his fucking mind!

"How do you propose we do that? We are on the other side of the world," Tayana asked throwing attitude. Jazz was about to answer when he noticed Joy, who had walked off with the people who they had been playing volleyball with, had returned and was lingering close by. Joy caught Tayana's eye and held her hand out with her five fingers spread. He knew how the game was played, if he had to guess she was silently telling Tayana she had to pay the volleyball players five-thousand dollars to shut them up about what they had witnessed with them and the guns. The absence of her second in command, Yolan, more than likely meant she was still 'sweet talking' the neighbors out of the phone. Him showing up like he did had just cost her five grand, but in his defense he had been telling the truth when he said he didn't know it was her people on the beach when he walked over. He thought he was surprising Tayana, not the entire crew.

Jazz watched the exchange as if he had no idea what was going on. He noticed the look of annoyance that skirted across Tayana's face as she sighed, picked up her bottled water taking a drink, and then shaking her head.

"Your girl Joy looks like she's ready to kill me," he said looking over at Joy again.

Tayana shrugged, watching Joy walk further down the beach and stopping to talk to the ladies still on the beach, casting mistrustful looks his way. "She is. After that rose stunt and now this, you will probably always be in her crosshairs so get used to it," she stated matter of factly.

"All the more reason to let me make it up to you. Let's have dinner," he offered, leaning a little closer to her. "You and I can spend some quality time together and your girls can see I'm not a bad guy and my interest in you is genuine," he added with a lopsided grin, she and that fucking smart ass mouth both annoyed and turned him on at the same time. He would play it cool for now because he knew she wasn't ready to be receptive to his way just yet, but she was really pushing it.

Tayana finished her water and put the empty bottle and her magazine back inside her bag. "Didn't you just say you were having dinner with your mama and the church ladies not even ten minutes ago?" Tayana asked, with her eyes narrowed suspiciously. "And, for the record, I can't believe you dragged your mama down here in order to stalk me," she snapped.

"I said my mom and her friends were watching a movie before dinner, Tayana. Not once did I say I was joining them. It's like this, once or twice a year I take her and her friends somewhere to relax and have fun. They shop, watch movies, and eat the crap they deprived themselves of for far too long. It had been a while since I'd done that and, since I was coming up here anyway, I invited them down. Yeah, I have to play their chauffeur, valet, and errand boy but it's a small price to pay especially after seeing you in that bathing suit, I have to say it is well worth it," he said, winking at her and licking his lips seductively. "And I'm not stalking you, Tayana. You said you had plans you couldn't break, I merely found a way to be a part of those plans," he explained with maddening logic. He knew his methods of pursuit were a bit unorthodox but with a woman like Tayana, taking control away from her was the only way to get what he knew they both wanted.

"Jazz, I must admit that is really sweet, the part about your mom, not you trying to strong arm your way into a date, Tayana said taking her sunglasses off and looking over at him.

He shrugged, staring down at her, his full bottom lip caught between his teeth as his eyes moved up her bikini-clad body. "Whatever it takes, right?" he said, looking back into her eyes. "Besides, when it comes to my mom, it's the least I could do, she's come a long way and been through a lot."

"I'm glad you feel that way, even though she is in recovery. A lot of people wouldn't see things that way, you know that once a fiend always a fiend mentality," Tayana said nodding thoughtfully looking out at the beach and sighing. "Regardless of what goes down, there is nothing like a mother's love and once she's gone, you are never the same," she said softly and thoughtfully.

Jazz kneeled in front of her and wiped away tears she probably didn't even realize had fallen from her eyes, before kissing her softly on the forehead. "I can't even imagine what that pain is like, Tayana, but I'm sure, wherever she is, she is proud of the woman you've become," he told her. He wanted, more than anything, to take her in his arms and hold her tight and love her through the pain she still obviously felt from her mother's death. But the way she dropped her head, quickly wiped her face before putting her sunglasses back on, her face set into a mask of indifference as she stared out at the water, he knew it wasn't an option, at least not yet.

Tayana?" he called her name softly when she was still quiet a few minutes later.

"Yes?" she answered, looking over at him through her dark sunglasses before looking back out towards the beach and water.

"Are you going to answer me about dinner, or am I just showing up at your door at eight and drag you somewhere kicking and screaming?" Jazz asked with a small chuckle.

Tayana pulled her gaze from the waves and focused on

him sighing again. "If you are nothing else you are persistent and you're too much, you know that, right?" she asked him while shaking her head and fighting back a smile.

"Yeah, I know I am and to think this is only the beginning, Beautiful," he replied reaching out and brushing a loose hair out of her face. He marveled at how beautiful she was again and the fact the more he was around her, the more she pulled him deeper under her spell without even realizing she was doing it.

"Fine, Jazz. I will join you for dinner." she said, finally letting her smile shine through as she reached up and brushed sand from his goatee. "Just know if you ever pull another stunt like this again, I might be forced to hurt you."

"Then get ready to hurt me, Tayana, because this is only the beginning."

"Thank you for dinner, Jazz., It was actually very nice," Tayana said walking next to Jazz on the beach, her sandals dangling from her fingertips. He'd taken her to a small seafood restaurant for dinner, and for once she had let her guard down around him a little bit and it felt good. She loved the way he looked at her and his subtle touches, it had been a long time since she felt so special. The wet sand smashed between her toes before the waves pushed in and washed it all away. The hem of her maxi sundress was soaked and she wondered when the last time was she had let herself relax this way and realized the feeling had everything to do with the drop-dead gorgeous man walking beside her.

"You are most welcome, Tayana. It was nice to see you, the real you for a change," Jazz said.

"I am always real, Jazz. I just don't like games or having

my time wasted." Tayana glared at him for a brief second. "I'm sure you, of all people, can understand that."

"I do understand, but I also know you are unlike any other woman I have ever met in the business, or not. The way you carry yourself and execute your moves is nothing short of amazing. You're just flawless."

Tayana stopped to look out at the water. "I'm not flawless, Jazz. I'm pretty far from it actually," she said, hating how his words of praise had made her feel. At that moment, she really didn't want to think about business, or remember who Jazz was and the threat he presented back home. For now she wanted to savor the enjoyment of his company, she didn't want to be 'Whisper', Heavy's daughter, determined to prove herself by any means necessary. For these last few minutes before she told Jazz goodnight she just wanted to be Tayana Bradley, Essie Bradley's baby girl and more than that she just wanted to be like any other woman who was attracted to a man.

Jazz moved until he was standing directly in front of Tayana. Slowly, he reached out and pulled her closer to him. She fit comfortably under his chin. After several awkward moments of standing in his arms with her arms locked at her side, she snaked her arms around his waist. They stood that way for the longest time, not talking, just slowly rocking in each other's arms.

It was exactly what she needed in that moment, almost as if he was reading her thoughts. She wasn't sure what side of Jazz she liked most, his demanding, bossy side or this tender, thoughtful side she had seen tonight. Just when she thought she had him pegged, he'd change up and show her a different side of his personality and she had to admit she couldn't wait to see what side he showed her next. Just when she started feeling like she could get used to being in his arms, she broke the spell. "Jazz, as nice as this has been, I have to say good night. I have early plans tomorrow with the ladies."

Tayana looked up into his handsome face and melted into his arms a little more, still not letting him go even though she knew she needed to.

"I hear what your mouth is saying, but I can feel what your body is shouting," Jazz said and leaned down capturing her mouth in a kiss. Soft and exploring at first, then he grabbed her to him, forcing his tongue into her mouth.

Tayana stood on her tiptoes and wrapped her arms around his neck, allowing her tongue to dance with his. Jazz leaned down and picked Tayana up off her feet, still kissing her.

He briefly pulled his lips away from hers and kissed her along her neckline and nipped her shoulder and collarbone. His panting breaths against her ear had her moaning out loud. Slowly he eased her down his body, she felt his erection pressing against her as he put her solidly back on her feet.

Jazz leaned down and pressed his lips to hers once more, most of his kisses had been forceful letting her know, in no uncertain terms, he wanted her and was claiming her for his own. This kiss was drastically different, it was softer with more passion behind it, letting her know without saying the words he didn't want the night to end. "Tayana, you know you're killing me out here right?" he asked her, touching her face when they broke apart.

Tayana reluctantly stepped out of the circle of his arms and turned to go up to the beach house. She saw Joy and Rini standing at the top of the hill and she wasn't lying she did have plans with the crew in the morning.

She turned back to look at him again, and said, "Not yet, Jazz. I will let you know when it's time to die."

Jazz watched Tayana slowly walking up the hill towards the house and away from him, his mind going a mile a minute, he suddenly realized what approach he needed to take with Tayana, none. He could tell from the last few minutes they spent together, and those few brief moments she spent in his arms, what she needed more than anything was calm. Time to let her hair down and not be in control, and that was exactly what he was going to make sure she had with him.

Chapter 5

Tayana walked downstairs, following her nose to the smell of breakfast the next morning. Her whole crew had banded together for another full day of fun in the sun.

"Oh, Sleeping Beauty's finally awake," Jaidyn teased, passing her a glass of freshly squeezed orange juice.

"What time is it anyway?" she asked while covering a yawn, grabbing the glass and snatching a piece of pineapple from the platter in the middle of the table.

"It's 10:30, hoochie! Joy told me all about you climbing up Jazz's tall ass last night!" Khyrs teased.

"And I know you a damn liar! Joy didn't tell you shit! Your nosy ass was peeking out the window to watch, huh? Bet money all y'all were!" Tayana laughed, taking a bite of her pineapple.

"Whatever you say, 'Boss Lady'!" Yolan screamed from her end of the table.

Tayana took a sip of her orange juice, shaking her head. "Y'all are going to get enough of calling me that shit!"

"Aww, look at her blush! So only Jazz can get away with calling you that?" Khyrs set a spinach and cheese omelet in front of her.

"No, it's equally annoying when he does it, now wipe it from your vocabulary." Tayana attempted to look serious and menacing but the minute she made eye contact with Monet she fell over laughing.

"Here, baby, eat your food, you need to keep your strength up if last night is an indicator of things to come!" Rini teased, handing her a fork.

Tayana took a bite of her omelet looking over at Rini in confusion. "What do you mean?"

"I'm talking about Jazz. That man stood on the beach staring up at the house for at least a damn hour. One kiss you got his ass sprung! You let him hit that and it's a wrap, he's gonna be calling you Boss Lady for real!" Rini answered, cutting into her own omelet.

"Whatever! I'm not naming no names, but who was that I heard singing soprano when I came in last night?" Tayana asked grabbing another slice of pineapple before looking down the table at all her ladies.

Shay blushed from the roots of her hair to the bottom of her feet. "You heard that, Whisper?" she asked softly.

"Shit! The whole house heard you, Shay!" Joy teased, taking her plate back to the kitchen.

"Sounds like S-Stuttering Butter is laying that pipe!" Yolan nudged Shay with her shoulder while taking a bite of a strawberry.

The rules were a bit more relaxed for this once yearly weekend. The ladies could fly their significant others in. All had been properly screened and were not a threat to the crew or business.

"All right, all right, ladies, enough of that, leave Shay alone. Let's finish up breakfast and get ready to ride some wave runners!" Tayana stood up and did a little dance with her hips before taking her plate to the kitchen.

"Yeah, I know what wave you want to ride," Yolan whispered when she slid into step next to her on the stairs.

"Yo, I swear you're pushing it," Tayana sang, going to her room to get dressed.

"Whisper?" Tayana 's gallery assistant, Sasha, knocked on her open office door.

Tayana looked up from her computer screen, her eyes widened in surprise for a brief moment. Her assistant, Sasha stood in her doorway holding an arrangement of Macro Dahlias, her favorite flower.

"These just came for you along with this." Sasha passed her a black envelope with gold music notes and a saxophone on the front of it. Inside was one ticket to the Cirque du Soleil Luzia.

Tayana put the ticket back in the envelope and indicated where on her desk Sasha could place the flowers.

"Thank you so much, Sasha. Are we busy in the showroom today?" Tayana asked, smiling at her assistant.

"Just mostly lookie-loos. Oh, yeah, I meant to talk to you, this one gentleman has been looking for 'Lock and Key' X-Change by WAK. I told him he could probably find it online but he wants us to order it, frame it, and deliver it to his office. I told him I needed to ask you first."

Tayana leaned forward and smelled one of the flowers. "Sash, we do that sort of thing all the time. Why would you need my permission to do that?"

Sasha shrugged. "Because he wants it in an African Black-wood frame and he wants you to deliver it."

Tayana looked up at Sasha with a frown. "The frame will be worth more than the print. Who does that?"

The doorbell in the showroom sounded. Sasha and Tayana both watched the monitor as an elderly black couple walked in.

"The same person who dropped off your flowers and that card. Anyway, I need to get back out front," Sasha said, walking out of her office to go help the new customers.

Tayana sat back shaking her head with a smile pulling out her phone, she had been wondering why he hadn't responded to her last text now she knew it was because he was waiting for his package to her to be delivered.

"Color me impressed, of course you would know what my favorite flower was. By the way what does one wear to the circus?" Tayana's text said the day after he got back from the Bahamas, he had stayed two days longer than she and her crew had. He was still in a pretty good mood after their date and from the look of things so was Tayana. They had talked every day since the night on the beach and where there was once only her snappish tone and sarcasm, now it had been replaced with sweet words and even a little teasing, asking him when she could see him again. Again his response had been a bit much and over the top but the girl had his nose open, had him thinking of new and creative ways to hold her attention. To be honest he was coming to realize Tayana bending to his will knocked him more off kilter than her 'Boss Lady' persona ever did.

"Jazz, like I said before, those females are banking and making money hand over fist. They ain't in our territory or even in our line of business per se, but with that much power it's only a matter of time until they are, we need to move on them," Slide said, looking across the massive desk at Jazz.

Jazz sent a quick text to Tayana before putting his phone face down on his desk and giving Slide his undivided attention. Slide, and his second in command, Reaper were having a brief meeting regarding a few new developments that had occurred when he was out of town.

Slide was one of his workers, he had been with Jazz longer than he could remember and usually his input and advice were welcomed, but he was like a dog with a bone regarding Tayana and her crew and Slide was getting on his damn nerves bringing them up all the damn time. He knew Slide had been feeling some type of way since the hit they executed on Raz and Jammy, but he needed to get over that shit. It was over and done with and everyone else involved had moved on.

"And I have already told you there is no reason for that, they aren't a threat to us in any way, shape, or form. I'm tired of talking about it so dead the conversation once and for all, you feel me?" Jazz asked Slide, his face set and deadly serious.

"Yeah, I feel you, Jazz," Slide answered, sitting back in his chair running his hand down his face impatiently. "Ay, are we finished here? I'm about to go handle some thangs on the West side," he asked, suddenly standing up and pulling out his phone.

Jazz's eyes narrowed for a split second before he nodded. "Yeah, you're good, go handle that. Check yourself, Slide, you're tap dancing on my nerves with that shit, last time I checked I'm the one making the calls here," Jazz told him, his light eyes flashing dark. One thing he had no patience for was disrespect and Slide was dangerously close to stepping into the territory at the moment.

Jazz and Reaper watched Slide nod in the affirmative before leaving his office, then they watched as he climbed into his Jaguar and drove away on the wall of monitors that were linked to the security cameras in front of Jazz's house.

"I don't know what's up with that fool lately, he has never

been so put out by another crew the way he is with Whisper and them. I hope his ass calms the hell down before I have to put something on him," Jazz said, shaking his head.

"You know how Slide gets down, Jazz. He barely respects women as it is, so to have a crew of all females do the slick shit they did at the club has him all in his feelings, he'll finish licking his wounds eventually. Speaking of Whisper, Cuzzo you sure you want to start up something with her? From what I've heard and what I saw, she is not the demure type," Reaper asked Jazz knowingly, watching for his reaction.

"Yeah, I know she's not but I'm going to anyway, something about her ha—" Jazz stopped talking suddenly and glared over at Reaper. "Damn, I can't stand your ass sometimes! How the hell did you even know that's where my head is at with her?" Jazz asked his cousin, shaking his head. An easy, knowing smile spread across Reaper's face.

"I know you better than anybody, Cuzzo. I saw this one coming a mile away, you been zeroed in on her since you met her. Just make sure you're thinking with the right head though, you can't afford to get sloppy with someone like her, Boss Lady ain't no joke." Reaper smirked using the nickname he heard Jazz call Tayana at least a dozen times.

"Well neither am I, which is why I am more than a little curious to see how we move together. It's been a minute since I even wanted to deal with a female on this level so you know when I choose, I'm going to choose wisely," Jazz replied, picking up his phone and smiling at the confirmation email and invoice from Essie's, slowly but surely day by day Tayana was coming closer to being all his.

"How much did Silvo say these were worth?" Punch asked, holding one of the 6-carat diamonds from his most recent shipment.

Tayana stood across from him in the frame room of the gallery. "$10,000 each."

Punch dropped the diamond back into the silk pouch to be with its 199 friends. "That's what's up. And the delivery fee?" he asked.

"As we previously discussed, getting conflict-free, but stolen, diamonds through customs would cost you $350,000 upon delivery."

Tayana placed her hands on her hips, Mary Jane rested at the small of her back.

Punch tied the pouch closed and tossed the diamonds to his partner at the door. "I'm thinking one," he replied with a smirk, sucking his teeth.

Tayana sighed, thinking to herself *here we go again, when will they ever learn?* It was always on their second business transaction. Once they discovered it was all ladies they were dealing with, they just had to try their luck. "The price just went up to $375,000 for wasting my time," Tayana said calmly, her hands still on her hips.

Punch sucked on his gold front tooth again puffing out his chest, clasping his hands in front of him. "I got my ice, I got my money, now you can take this one and be okay with it 'cause you ain't got shit else, bitch!" he spat, looking Tayana up and down like he smelled something foul.

Tayana smiled with an icy glare in Punch's direction just as his partner dropped to the cement floor with a bullet hole in his head from Rini's gun, *Sugar Baby*. "Strike one," she counted quietly moving closer to Punch's partner.

Punch's smile disappeared, Tayana could smell the fear on him, the little punk! *Who's the bitch now?* she thought smugly.

Tayana looked down at her suit, small droplets of blood were now sprinkled on the shoulder of her jacket, her slacks and blouse were clean. Blood pooled around her custom Jimmy Choo's. She reached down and took the silk pouch from his partner's dead hand and discreetly pulled Mary Jane from her ankle holster.

"Now you owe me $425,000 plus $10,000 for my one-of-a-kind suit and shoes, and $15,000 for wasting my time," she declared, sounding far more patient than she actually felt. She wanted to punch his ass in the throat for fucking with her time and ruining her suit, she really liked this one, and don't even get her started on her shoes, *fuck!*

Punch was still looking around for the invisible gunman, or in this case gun woman, but attempted to play tough yet again. "375! Yo, what about my ice, bitch!"

Tayana walked up, pulled Mary Jane up from her side, and shot out Punch's right kneecap. "Strike two and *my* ice, *bitch.* You have two days to get me my money," Tayana told him and moved towards the door.

"Man! Fuck you, Whisper! I ain't giving you shit, you man hating cunt! Trick ass bitch!" Punch sobbed out, clutching his bloody knee.

Tayana shot him in the face from across the room, while standing in the doorway before stepping over his dead partner.

"Strike three. Why is the word *bitch* always the first thing that tumbles out of their fucking mouths when they don't get their way? So unnecessary, I swear." She sighed walking up to Rini and Joy.

"Call for a cleanup and toss their spot, then make it disappear. Our price is now $500,000 for the inconvenience this caused on top of the original price of the diamonds," Tayana instructed and took off her suit jacket and tossed it back into the frame room.

"Whisper, what about the shoes?" Joy asked as Tayana moved through the cement basement to the back exit.

Tayana slipped her shoes off and held them in her hand after tucking Mary Jane back into her ankle holster. "I will handle them myself, shoes this pretty deserve a proper burial, I guarantee tears will be shed."

"Are you going to go?" Yolan asked Tayana, while sipping her *Ketel One* martini.

Tayana was still wound up after her meeting with Punch and asked Yolan to join her for a drink after going home to change. The remainder of her one-of-a-kind suit and shoes were now a charred memory.

"Yeah I'm going to go but I still don't know what to do about this budding relationship as a whole, I have a business to run. I do not have time for a man like Jazz," she said, sipping her white wine, sitting back in the bar's plush chair.

"Tay, your business is a well-oiled machine three times over. Your team is loyal and well taken care of and you are a fuckin' *boss*. Stop tripping and let that man knock those knees loose!" Yolan told her, winding her hips in her chair.

Tayana actually spit out her wine. "Yolan, you are a damn fool! For the record, Jazz is a boss, I am a businesswoman," she said, dabbing her silk blouse with a cloth napkin.

"Tomato, potato! Shit, that man is fine as hell, you said you two had fun at dinner, you have been talking to him daily since we got back and did I mention the man is fine as hell?" Yolan asked with a wicked grin.

"Yes, Yo, I believe you mentioned the man was fine," Tayana said rolling her eyes at Yolan.

"Let the man spoil you, Tay, show you what it's like when a man is interested in you. Because, honestly, I believe you have forgotten. You already know if he comes foul, your Lovely Lethals got your back," Yolan reasoned, signaling their server for another round.

A few days later, Jazz was standing outside the event center in front of the main entrance when Bruise pulled up to drop Tayana off for their date.

"Whisper, you want me to check things out before you get out?" Bruise asked in typical big brother mode. He was overprotective of all of them.

"B, you know how I do. I will be fine. The Firm is here so technically you, Joy, and Rini will be with me all night," she said, hoping for the hundredth time that agreeing to see Jazz again didn't turn out to be a mistake.

Bruise stepped out of the car and walked around to open her door. He chucked his head in Jazz's direction with the universal sign for 'what's up'.

Jazz nodded in Bruise's direction, his hands were clasped in front of him. His black jeans hugged his muscular legs perfectly. He was in a black button-down shirt and suit jacket, and black suede sneakers. Even dressed down, he looked ready for the runway.

"Tayana, I'm glad you could make it," Jazz said, stepping up and helping her out of the backseat of her car before guiding her into the venue.

She noticed two of The Firm guards right away at the box seating entrance and felt herself relax a bit.

"Thank you for inviting me. I have never been to a circus in my life," Tayana admitted. Her mother hated things like zoos and circuses. Her father never really spent a lot of his leisure time with her, only with her brothers, so when she wasn't hanging out with Yolan and their crew, she was busy studying and plotting their come up.

"Well, then you are in for a treat." Jazz showed her to their seats. Their box was empty except for them.

Tayana scanned the other boxes and immediately clocked his security, they were seated on either side of their box, looking out of place compared to the other people in their boxes. He also had two sets of men in every section on the main floor.

"Can't wait." Tayana sat back with a smirk. Maybe one day she would tell him how bad his guys were at blending in, maybe even offer up lessons from The Firm to help them do better.

Jazz watched Tayana more than he watched the performance, the way her face lit up excitedly as she watched everything let him know he'd made the right choice in choosing to take her there and in his assumption on the beach. She was so damn busy handling things, she never took the time to have fun. Bringing her over to his way of thinking was going to be easier than he initially thought, he just had to make sure she was like she was right now, relaxed with her guard down.

"Did you enjoy the performance?" Jazz asked across the candlelit table; they decided on a after the show. Tayana actually rode with him to the restaurant, something about Jazz had her breaking all of her rules and she wasn't sure how she felt about that. Even though she was actually having a good time with Jazz she still didn't know him enough to trust him yet.

"It was really beautiful, all the colors and attention to

detail was amazing. Thank you for inviting me." Tayana took a sip of her sparkling water with lime, smiling over at him. "Oh, I forgot, thank you for the flowers. Macro Dahlias are my favorites, I won't even ask how you knew that."

Jazz watched her as she licked the excess water from her bottom lip. He shifted uncomfortably as he began to harden just from that simple act. "Anytime. I'm glad you liked them and the show, you are a hard woman to impress, Tayana," he replied, his eyes sparkling in the candlelight.

Tayana smiled, looking down at the menu. "I have yet to fully understand what it is about me, besides a physical attraction, that makes you feel so inclined to try and impress me at all. Anyway, does anything look good to you?" she asked smiling over at him again.

Jazz reached across the table and took her hand. "It's more than that, Tayana and by now you know that as well as I do. Stop trying to play your little head games or I promise you will not like the outcome. In answer to your question, the only thing that looks good to me in here, at the moment, is you," he said with a grin that had her ready to drop her thong at his feet.

Tayana's eyes met his across the table as he ran his thumb softly across the top of her hand. His light eyes were pulling her in, giving her a fever. When he ran his tongue across his lip, her first thought was to say they should skip dinner and find a place to feast on each other instead, but in true Tayana form, she resisted. "I meant on the menu, Jazz."

He shrugged. "Doesn't matter what I eat, I would rather be tasting you so why don't you pick something that you like?" he suggested with the same grin.

Tayana grabbed her water and took a big drink, blushing while trying to check her hormones. This man was killing her resolve. "You sure you want to trust me to do that, Jazz?" she asked clearing her throat and pulling her eyes from his and looking back down at the menu and back at him again. She couldn't help it! She could get lost in those sexy ass eyes!

Jazz took a drink from his highball glass, his eyes still on her. "Yes, Tayana, I trust you," he answered without hesitation. "I trust you until you give me a reason not to. Don't ever give me a reason not to trust you, Tayana. It won't be pretty." His eyes flashed dark before his flirty demeanor and smile returned.

Tayana's heart skipped a beat as she stared over at Jazz. The fact he always called her by her real name felt more intimate than a kiss every time he said it, even his veiled warning had her feeling hot and bothered, oh hell, naw! She was tripping for real!

Tayana fought to rein in her hormones again and called their waiter over and ordered fire-grilled shrimp and scallops, asparagus in lemon caper sauce, and rice pilaf for both of them.

"I guess I should have asked you if you even like seafood. I hope you do?" Tayana asked, blushing a little bit at the oversight and at the low-lidded gaze on his face that was talking straight to her middle.

Jazz sat back in his chair and smiled that sexy ass smile of his. "I told you it doesn't matter, you are what I really want to eat so unless you are on that menu, I might as well be eating cotton," he replied, while his eyes ran up and down her body slowly. In that moment it was more intimate than a caress.

It was after eleven. Their plates had been cleared and they still sat making small talk.

"Jazz, you know this place closes at midnight, right? We should get going, call it a night," Tayana grudgingly said, finishing her third glass of sparkling water.

"I know, but I have to be honest. I don't want this to end, I'm really enjoying your company." Jazz reached across the table grabbing Tayana's hand again.

"Me either, Jazz. But we have to, it's getting late." Tayana slowly pulled her hand from his grasp and stood to pull on her jacket.

Jazz stood and walked over to assist her. Once she had it on, he pressed his front against her back holding her close. His arms circled her waist as his growing erection rested against the small of her back. He dropped a soft kiss on her neck. Tingles climbed up Tayana's legs and landed between her thighs, awakening her second heartbeat.

"Stay the night with me, Tayana," he whispered against her ear before running his tongue around it.

Tayana stepped out of his arms and grabbed her purse, ignoring his request.

"Tayana, do you trust me?" Jazz asked untucking his shirt to cover his erection. His eyes low and dark with desire and too much cognac.

Tayana stared at him without blinking and fought her screaming hormones. Her common sense took over as it usually did and she reminded herself who she was, who he was and what could possibly happen when she let her guard down around the wrong man. Her suspicious mind immediately led her thoughts to Thirst, her first and only love.

The man she gave her virginity and her loyalty to, the man who almost killed her.

In that instant she wasn't sure if she was ready for Jazz and all he was trying to offer her but she wanted to be, so it made her next words extremely hard to say.

"No, Jazz, I'm sorry but I don't trust you, at least not yet but believe me when I say I really want to and for me that speaks volumes. I want you like I have never wanted any man before in my life but I know in my heart that tonight just isn't the night to move in that direction and if I tried to force it and ignore the misgivings I still have it would end all bad and I don't want that." She explained nervously, hoping her admission and words were not the cause for him to end their budding romance. She knew what she said wasn't what he wanted to hear but she had to be honest, if what she was beginning to feel for Jazz was the real thing she needed to be able to give herself to him 100% and as long as she still had doubts there was just no way to do that.

"Tayana, I don't know what more I can do or say to show you my feelings for you are genuine as are my intentions but what I do know is, I can't keep running into the same wall climbing over it each time we see each other. I want you. I want to be with you, I want to build something with you but I can't be the only one moving towards those goals. You say you're not ready for the next step in our relationship I respect that and I'm going to respectfully step away to give you your time to think things through, the next move is yours," Jazz told her tipping her head back and leaning down kissing her softly on the lips before taking her hand and walking her out the restaurant, Bruise pulled up from the end of the parking lot a few moments later.

"Goodnight, Tayana," he said touching her face lightly after helping her get inside of her car and closing the door.

"Have a good time, Whisper?" Bruise asked when they pulled from the curb.

Tayana stared out the car window at Jazz, who had just passed his ticket to the valet for his car, he stared back before flashing her his sexy ass smile and winked, his hands were in his pockets.

Tayana sat back and closed her eyes, tears of regret wanted to fall. "Yeah, B, it was nice." Her hormones and the heartbeat between her legs were screaming at her for letting them down but she knew she made the right decision. After all of these years she still wasn't over the pain of betrayal Thirst put her through. And she didn't want Jazz paying for another man's mistakes she needed to be able to come to him just like he was coming to her, she just had to figure out how to do that before she lost him for good.

Chapter 6

"You ou mean to tell me you walked away from that sexy ass man again, Whisper?" Joy asked her the next morning as she held out the focus mitts for Tayana to hit.

After a sleepless night, Tayana met Joy in the gym at 5:30 a.m. to work off all the sexual frustration she felt.

"Joy, you of all people must understand why I did. You know who he is, and what that can mean for us if he's trying to get over on me in some fucked up power move," she argued, swinging her fists at the focus mitts, irritated as hell at her hormones and little lady for calling out to Jazz all night long.

"Is he trying to get over on you, Whisper?" Joy asked, dropping her hands and looking pointedly at Tayana.

With nothing for Tayana to hit she started to pace back and forth. Tayana knew and almost hated the answer, Jazz Jones was genuinely interested in her and made no qualms about making sure she knew it. All the excuses she kept throwing up about protecting the crew and who he was in the business world were exactly that, just excuses. She knew how to handle shady ass people, and especially shady ass men, but a straight up one, she really didn't know how to handle.

"No, Joy. No, he's not," Tayana admitted pulling off her gloves and sitting down on the mat.

Joy dropped the focus mitts and sat down next to her. "So then what's next, Whisper?"

Tayana dragged her hand down her face before letting out a frustrated groan. "I have no fucking idea!" she screamed and lay back on the mat.

"So the apartments in this high-rise are so clean, Tay. I think you might want to consider buying a few of the new ones, real estate in this area is popping right now," Yolan informed Tayana, passing her a listing of the same property she had pulled up on her computer.

Yolan had called to set up a meeting to discuss some of the new listings that were available and knew might pique Tayana's interest. They'd also be a good investment for the crew.

Tayana sat across from Yolan, staring out of the window, and idly playing with her lip. Her mind was still on Jazz and what she was going to do about him, one minute she wanted to believe he was everything he appeared to be and let her guard down, the next minute all she could think was he was too good to be true and was going to try and get over on her.

Another sleepless night had her mind all over the place which pissed her off even more, her thoughts always lined up perfectly with what she was in the process of doing at the time. Two dates and Jazz had managed to get under her skin, messing with her peace of mind, she was not okay.

"Tay! Where you at?" Yolan asked loudly, slapping her palm on her desk.

The sound made Tayana jump and shift her attention back to Yolan. "I'm so sorry, Yo. What were you saying?" she asked, looking down at the listing in her hand.

"Shelf that, what's going on with you? You haven't really been 'here' since you got here," Yolan said, standing up and grabbing her coffee cup to refill it. "You want a cup? Naw, you already look too amped and wired. Imma bring your ass a cup of tea and then you can tell me what the hell is going on," Yolan declared, walking out of her office and over to the coffee station in the lobby.

"Where's Neutral at today?" Tayana asked, noticing that Yolan's business partner and one of their other best friends, Asia wasn't there like she usually was when they went over listings. Asia's nickname was Neutral because she was just that, neutral. She was part of the crew but she wasn't 'in' the crew. Tayana sighed and finally actually started reading the listing in her hands instead of just staring at the pictures.

"She's on vacation, remember? Her and Butchie went to Jamaica for a week, their 'first time meeting' anniversary is this week. Seriously, Tay what's going on with you, girl? You never forget stuff like this." Yolan handed Tayana a coffee cup with a tea bag floating in it and took her seat behind her desk.

"I'm good, Yo, it just slipped my mind. We have so much going on, I guess my mental rolodex is on the fritz. This high-rise is fire, what's the asking price on the apartments there?" Tayana asked, taking a sip of her tea and putting the cup on a coaster on Yolan's desk.

Yolan sat up and stared at Tayana like she was crazy. "Heffa, who the fuck do you think you're talking to? You know good and damn well I know you better than you know your damn self! You, Miss Tayana Bradley, do not forget dates and you damn sure don't forget where your ladies are at any given time so miss me with that. You also just sipped hot water because the tea hasn't had time to brew yet so, like I said a few minutes ago, spill it," Yolan demanded, sitting back in her chair, crossing her legs, clutching her coffee cup.

Tayana dragged her eyes from the listing to Yolan's face. "Yo, I don't even know what's wrong with me lately, this shit with Jazz has really thrown me off my game! I can't sleep and during the day I can't focus because I'm thinking about him, I mean what am I, twelve?" Tayana snapped, picking up the flavor tag on her tea bag in her cup and dunking it a few times before taking it out and tossing it in the trash can next to Yolan's desk. "Oh, and do you know Joy told me she won't spar with me in the mornings anymore until I figure out what I want to do about Jazz, she said I'm driving her crazy talking in circles about him."

"Tay, I have to agree with Joy. You're being ridiculous, you either want to date the man or you don't. You can't have it both ways and we can't have you off your game either, it's dangerous for all of us," Yolan said, sipping her coffee now that it was cool enough to drink.

"Yolan, you of all people know what I've been through and why after that nightmare of an experience I would be spooked by someone showing any kind of romantic interest in me, especially someone in our line of work," Tayana reasoned, picking up the listings they were meeting about, and hoping Yolan would catch the hint she didn't want to dive deeper into this subject at the moment.

"I feel you, Tay and if you're not ready for things to head in the direction he wants things to, then you need to tell him, it's not fair to play with his emotions." Yolan pulled up the listing Tayana was looking at on her computer again. "And to answer your previous question, the apartments in that high-rise are going for $550,000 to $850,000 depending on the square footage and the floor they're on."

Tayana studied the amenities and floor plans again biting the inside of her cheek. "Buy six, we can rent out three and have the other three furnished and on standby if we need them, anything else?"

Yolan set her cup down and scribbled down a few notes before looking at Tayana again. "Yeah just one thing, I want you to know it's okay for you to be happy, Tayana. There is so much more to life than just handling business, you gotta start understanding that, Tay. I know you hate to hear it, but I wouldn't be a good friend if I wasn't real with you. Tay, it's time for you to let go of the past and realize it's not Jazz you don't trust, it's yourself." Yolan reached across the desk and took Tayana's hand, tears danced in her eyes.

"Damn it, Yolan, why did you have to get all emotional and shit? Knowing good and damn well I'm just as emotional, you cry, I cry." Tayana quickly wiped her tears away. "I'm just so scared, Yo. The last time almost cost us both our lives. I can handle someone hurting me but someone hurting one of my ladies? My sisters in sin? Naw, I ain't having it," Tayana admitted and grabbed a tissue from the box on Yolan's desk.

"What do you always tell us, Tay? Fear is a wasted emotion, it clouds your judgment and messes with your common sense. You're stronger and smarter than you were then and be honest, Tay, Jazz is nothing like Thirst and you know it."

That was one of the many reasons she loved Yolan and all of her ladies the way she did, yeah she was the boss and did not tolerate disrespect, but if she was wrong they let her know and often with her own damn words of wisdom.

"True but honestly, Yo, I don't know what he's like yet. I've been so busy waiting for him to show his true intentions, I haven't paid attention to the man he really is." Tayana wiped away a few more tears looking over at Yolan sheepishly.

Yolan drank the rest of her coffee and grabbed the listings from Tayana. "Then I strongly suggest you do, and sooner rather than later. Until then can you get your emotional gangsta ass out of my office please? I have a potential client coming in about fifteen minutes and if she sees you here tearing, and snotting, and shit she might turn heel and run." Yolan scoffed coming from behind her desk with her arms outstretched.

"Whatever, Yo, you started this crying mess, not me, and thanks for calling me on my shit." Tayana stood up and hugged Yolan tight for a few minutes before she let her go and held her at arm's length. "You know you tell anyone I was in here whining about a man, Imma have to kill you, right?" she threatened jokingly.

Yolan scoffed again. "Girl, please, we all know you've been whining over that damn man, why do you think I called you here for a meeting instead of just sending you an email? I drew the short straw and had to take one for the team and talk to your evil ass!" she informed her, rolling her eyes.

Tayana's eyes widened in surprise. "Seriously, Yo? I'm that bad?" Tayana knew she brought Jazz up a few times, like when she was at the shop getting her hair done by Khyrs the other day, or when she was getting a final fitting with Monet and Shay for her newest suit, to replace the one she had to get rid of after her meeting with Punch, and of course, when she was working out in the mornings with Joy. Okay she brought him up more than a few times, she really was constantly talking about him, well damn.

"Chile please! You have the man's name and stats on repeat so much we can all quote them verbatim!" Yolan snapped, walking her to the door. "Now stop telling us about him and go talk to him. Put him and us all out of our misery!"

———

Tayana paced nervously in front of the blanket she had spread by the lake in Lyndale Park a few hours before sunset two weeks later.

That's how long it took her to muster up the courage to talk to Jazz, she emailed Jazz an invitation to meet her in her favorite park to talk. He sent her his trademark business card with gold music notes and a saxophone as a reply. No words or anything just the card, so she held out hope that was his way of accepting her invite, she even had Ms. Lanie make up a picnic meal to share before they walked through the gardens.

"I don't know, Mo. I'm going to wait about fifteen more minutes and then I'm going to head out," Tayana said to Monet over the phone, feeling stupid. She finally put herself out there and she had no idea if it was for nothing or not.

"Whisper, you need to chill, you said 5:30, it's barely 5:00, not everyone in the world is as overly punctual as we all are," Monet reasoned. Tayana could hear her moving pots around, meaning she was about to cook something.

Monet could throw down, she was the best cook in the crew, the only person who gave her a run for her money was the greatest cook they knew, Ms. Lanie.

"True, but it's not like he even really told me he was coming, he just sent me that damn card and did I tell you about the WAK he ordered? The fucking frame is worth more than the damn print!" Tayana fussed just because she could.

"Whisper, you sent the man home with blue balls three times now, can you blame the man if he is being cautious or making your evil ass sweat a little?" Monet chuckled.

"Whatever, Monet, and I know you heffas ain't over there having eggplant parmesan without me!" Tayana snapped, looking up at the black-on-black Jaguar F-type that just pulled up in the parking lot, the pretty ass car screamed Jazz Jones.

He stepped out of the car in his regular GQ style. From where she was standing she could see he was wearing jeans again, a button-down shirt, and Gucci sunglasses. Even from a distance he took her breath away and she couldn't help the smile that crept across her face.

"Whisper, are you good?" Monet yelled into the phone.

Tayana turned her back, so she would stop staring at Jazz as he approached, and focused on her phone call. "Shit, Mo, I'm sorry. My bad what did you just say?" she asked Monet, trying to stop grinning like a damn fool.

"I said no, we aren't having eggplant parmesan without you, we're having chicken parmesan without you and he must be there because I can hear your ass grinning through the damn phone. Just let what's going to happen with you two happen, Whisper," Monet said. Tayana could tell she was smiling too.

"I'll try Mo and you heffas better save me some damn food!" she teased looking over her shoulder as Bruise walked towards her with Jazz a few steps behind him.

Shatter, Trench and Cisco from The Firm were stationed further down the path from where she had set up for their picnic, she was sure he'd brought security detail with him too, the fact of the matter was they were who they were and in a public park.

"You know we will and have fun, get out of your head for a little while," Monet instructed, "And remember your Lovely Lethals got your back, we won't let a thing happen to you 'Boss Lady'!"

Tayana heard screams of laughter from the rest of the crew as she hung up.

Tayana dropped her phone in her Chanel handbag and turned around as she watched in amusement as Jazz gingerly stepped across the grass trying not to ruin his tennis shoes. She thought she was bad about her shoes, but Jazz had her beat.

"Boss Lady, long time, no see," he said once he was

standing directly in front of her. His face gave nothing away, this might as well have been the first time they met.

Bruise gave Tayana a meaningful look to let her know he'd still be close by and walked back towards the parking lot.

"I wasn't sure you'd come, but I had Ms. Lanie prepare a picnic. I hope you're hungry," she said, noticing instantly he had gone back to calling her that annoying ass nickname, looking up at him nervously she had missed him so much and hoped she wasn't too late and he would be receptive to hearing her out. The fact she was actually nervous really disturbed her. It was easier to deal with him when she thought he was up to no good

"I am, but before we sit down to eat, we need to talk, both of us. Not just me opening up and you listening, making mental notes and inventing new reasons not to trust me," he replied, still standing in front of her looking at her, he had yet to smile.

Tayana sighed and fought the urge to say something smart, he was right after all. She spent most of her time observing people, cataloging their weaknesses in case she needed to expose them later on, other than her ladies no one really knew much about her, not even what her favorite color was.

"Yes, Jazz, as I said in my invitation, I wanted to meet up to clear the air and talk. Since it was me who extended the invitation I naturally assumed I would be doing most of the talking," she said, while walking over to the down comforter she had set up in the grass.

"I have to say, I never pictured you as the picnic type, Boss Lady," he quipped, watching her slip off her shoes and settling down on the blanket. "Bugs, dirt, and grass just don't seem like your thing."

She looked up at him while she used a cloth napkin to clean the grass from the heels of her shoes, she purposely wore a simple pair of Chanel pumps she didn't mind getting dirty. This was no place for her Jimmy Choos or Louboutins.

"Hmm, from the look of things it appears you're having more of a problem with it than I am, Jazz." She carefully set her shoes on the side of the blanket and opened the basket Ms. Lanie had packed.

Tayana could already tell Ms. Lanie had gone overboard, she pulled out each container and set it on the blanket, there was sliced watermelon, strawberries, red and green grapes, spinach salad, caprese salad, ambrosia salad, macaroni salad, carved chicken and turkey breasts, four kinds of cheeses both cubed and sliced, lettuce and tomatoes, sliced croissants for sandwiches, olives, pickles and even a small white chocolate and raspberry cake for dessert, one of Tayana's very favorite desserts.

"Are you going to have a seat and join me or are you going to just stand there looking at the grass like you're going to kill it if it messes up your shoes?" Tayana asked, pulling out the condiments and dishes from the basket.

"Both and shit, good thing I am hungry, whoever this Ms. Lanie is, she packed enough to feed half this damn park." Jazz finally slipped off his shoes and joined her on the blanket.

Tayana handed him a plastic warming pouch with a wet hand towel in it, as well as the cloth napkin she used for her shoes. "For your hands and your shoes, I would hate to be responsible for grass stains on your shoes," she said with a smirk opening up her own pouch and washing her hands.

She watched Jazz clean off his shoes while she organized the containers of food on the blanket. Her smile came easy when he opened his pouch and pulled out the still warm towel with a look of surprise. "If you are nothing else, you are all class, Boss Lady," Jazz told her washing his hands with the towel, a small smile on his face.

"Thanks, I think? But this is all courtesy of Ms. Lanie, she likes to make a good impression." Tayana handed him a plate and silverware.

"The people you surround yourself with are often a reflection of you, so if Ms. Lanie is this classy it's because she is working for you and you exude nothing but class," he argued, grabbing the container of grapes and putting several on his plate.

"Duly noted, now I have to ask a very crucial question, I'm talking make or break here, are you a dill pickle or sweet pickle person?" She held up both containers waiting for him to tell her his preference.

"Ain't no way in hell I'm a sweet pickle person, I was born and raised in the Lone Star State, you better ask somebody." Jazz grabbed the container of dill pickles and put one on his plate, Tayana sat watching him, grinning like she had won the lottery.

Once they both fixed their food, they settled into casual silence watching the swans move across the lake next to them. Every time she looked up from her plate his eyes were on her, thoughtful.

"So, Boss Lady, you said we were going to talk, so talk," Jazz said setting his plate to the side.

Tayana took a bite of the strawberry in her hand and chewed thoughtfully, not sure of where she should begin, so she just shrugged and started talking.

"Jazz, I'm sorry for blowing so hot and cold with you. Being a woman in our line of work, I have to be doubly careful. Me and my crew worked so hard to build what we have and I can't let anyone come in trying to sabotage that."

Tayana saw his jaw begin to work as he ground his teeth, he didn't say anything just used his napkin to brush crumbs off of his lap as he waited for her to continue talking.

"I honestly don't know where I want this thing between us to go but I do know I really enjoy your company and want to get to know you better." Tayana pulled out the plastic bag Ms. Lanie packed in the basket for their trash and began cleaning up their mess. "I hope you can understand my need to take things a little slow, it's not just about me losing everything I've worked for but my ladies too."

Jazz reached out and grabbed her hand and stopped her from cleaning up their picnic.

"First of all let me say this, I knew exactly all I needed to know about you and your crew before I even sent you that drink the night we met, so if my intention was to wreck your shit, Whisper, I would have done it already. I move quick and react even quicker, you and your ladies would still be trying to figure out what the fuck happened. I know you are all about the smooth and quiet execution but being who I am, I don't handle business that way. These streets know me and know what I'm about so I let my rep do more talking than I do in that regard. Secondly, you keep acting like you're the only one who loses if shit goes bad with us, you're not, I have more to lose than you do. Lastly, let me be clear, Tayana my interest in you has *nothing* to do with business and everything to do with me being attracted to you, period. Now you can either rock with that, see where this thing takes us or let me know so I can stop running into the same damn brick wall and wasting my time," he told her sternly before reaching out and touching her face. "The ball is in your court, so you tell me what game we're about to play."

Tayana silently absorbed what he said and went back to clearing up the trash from their picnic. He made a lot of good points and, in normal circumstances, she would be a little more than upset by what he said about her and her ladies and taken it as a threat, but if she was going to trust Jazz, she needed to start somewhere.

She dropped down on her knees in front of him and pulled his sunglasses from his face. "Well, Jazz, I've always been a slow learner when it came to games so why don't you tell me and I follow your lead?" She leaned forward and gently pressed her lips to his.

"Whisper, the WAK is here, the frame came out beautiful don't you think? Anyway, I told him you would deliver it after the gallery closes today." Sasha walked into her office and set Jazz's print on the display stand in her office corner a week later.

She and Jazz had spent a lot of time together in the last month, he took her to his favorite place, a jazz club he owned downtown, she took him to hers, The Museum of Fine art. They had lunch dates, went to a couple of shows and even went to the gun range together. Tayana was having a good time with Jazz but still slipped away and went home every time things got hot and heavy, she just wasn't ready to let him all the way in just yet.

Tayana looked from the print to Sasha, confused. "I'm doing what after the gallery closes?"

Sasha looked at her with her eyebrow raised. It was usually Tayana who was reminding her of special instructions, not the other way around. "You good, Whisper? Remember, I told you about this? It was the day the first flowers came," she stated, her gaze went to her newest arrangement of macro dahlias and roses.

The dahlias were shades of dark purples and pale pinks this time, the roses were true blood black roses – roses with red centers and black tips on the petals – the arrangement was hauntingly beautiful and unique. He had sent her flowers every day since their picnic in the park and the arrangements were never the same outside of the macro dahlia's being the focal point of each one.

Tayana sat back rolling her pen between her fingers staring at the print. A nude man and woman embracing one another. The man is holding a keyring with a heart-shaped lock, the woman holds a keyring with the key for the lock.

"Yeah, I'm good, Sash, but you are going to have to deliver it. I have a meeting tonight," Tayana said, looking over at her new flowers and its calling card. Black with gold music notes and a saxophone, she knew she didn't have it in her to resist Jazz even one more time.

She wanted the man so bad she could taste it and had run out of excuses of why she needed to leave when it was obvious she wanted to stay.

"No can do, Whisper. He was very insistent, since the beginning, that you had to be the one to deliver it or no sale. And before you say, 'so what?', please bear in mind that frame? It cost $25,000." Sasha leaned on the doorframe with her arms folded looking at Tayana.

Tayana dropped her pen on her desk and sat up hard. "$25,000? Is he crazy?" Tayana walked over to the print and touched the beautiful dark wood.

Sasha stood up straight and shrugged. "Maybe you should ask him when you deliver it." Sasha quickly moved back out the door and down the hall towards the showroom, before Tayana could put up more of a fight.

Tayana turned and watched Sasha retreating down the hall biting the inside of her cheek. "Well played, Mr. Jones. Well played. Shit!" She sighed as she logged into her computer to look up his email to arrange an exact delivery time.

———

"Whisper, are you sure you don't want me to drive you to deliver it?" Bruise asked following her to the garage after the gallery closed that night.

Tayana carefully placed the print in the back of her pearl white Land Rover and closed the hatch slowly. "No, B, I will be okay. Joy and Rini will be close just in case, and Mary Jane too." Tayana lifted her pant leg showing Bruise her holstered best friend.

"All right then, Whisper. You know if anything jumps off, I'm a phone call away."

Tayana pulled into the driveway of the house in Piney Point Village, cussing Jazz smooth the fuck out in her head. He told her she was delivering the print to his office not his fucking house!

She took a few deep breaths and scanned the property. Security cameras and motion detection lighting but no security detail. This was his home, not the house where his business was conducted. She wanted to kill him!

"Are you going to get out of the car or what?" Jazz asked, tapping on the passenger's window smiling.

Tayana narrowed her eyes in his direction before sliding out of the car.

"You lied." Was all she said as she walked to the back of her car to grab the print.

He frowned as he met her there from the passenger's side. "I lied? Exactly what are you talking about, Tayana?" he asked, looking both triumphant and smug.

Tayana rolled her eyes and pulled the print from the Rover. "You told me this print was to be delivered to your office. This is not your office." Tayana jerked away when he tried to take the print from her.

"Tayana, I never lied to you. This is for my office. My home office. Please let me help you carry that inside." Jazz reached for the print again.

Tayana jerked away again and moved up the driveway towards the house. "I got it," she snapped already feeling herself getting wet. It didn't matter what the man wore, he looked like her perfect meal and she was fucking *starving*!

The print was huge but she was determined to carry it to his office out of spite. When they reached the foyer, Jazz reached from behind her and grabbed the framed print with one hand. "A hard head makes for a sore behind, Tayana, remember that," he admonished in a low menacing voice.

Tayana whirled around. "Careful, Jazz, you do realize you paid $25,000 for that frame right?" she asked him, ignoring his warning. The art lover in her was all about protecting the print and frame.

Jazz held the print out studying it for a brief moment. "It's perfect." He nodded at it and smiled over at Tayana looking impressed. "You do good work, Tayana."

"Well, we aim to please. I'm glad you like it. Good night, Jazz." Tayana turned to make a quick getaway when he reached out and touched her arm.

"Isn't there an installation guarantee or something like that at Essie's? I mean come on, $25,000 frame? It would be a shame if I ruined it, right?" Jazz smiled over at her, knowing she would cave.

Tayana closed her eyes and blew out a deep breath. "Lead the way, Jazz." Knowing every minute she was in Jazz's house her resolve was chipping away to nothing, she foolishly relented to walk deeper inside of the lion's den.

He smiled even bigger as he began to walk from the great room and to the right, still admiring the print.

He was in a button-down shirt that was open to the last three buttons, his sleeves were rolled up. His jeans had her mouth watering with the way they fit. She was so busy staring at his ass as he led the way to his office that she bumped into him from behind when he stopped walking.

"You good back there?" he asked, chuckling, looking over his shoulder at her knowingly.

"I'm fine. I just mis-stepped." Tayana blushed and moved from behind him and into the office.

It was full of office furniture all made out of African Blackwood, no wonder he chose it for the frame.

She lightly ran her fingers across the desk as she passed it looking for the perfect spot to hang the print.

"Well, I guess my first question is do you want this to just tie into the decor of the room or be the focal point?"

Jazz was watching her, still standing just inside the door of his office. His eyes were traveling up and down her body, she could just about tell where his thoughts were.

Tayana waved her hands in front of his face to get his attention. "Hello? Jazz, where do you want it?" she asked before turning back around, looking at the wall space behind his desk.

Jazz moved into the office until he was standing behind her. "Where do you want it, Tayana?"

Tayana looked over her shoulder at him. His eyes darkened as he looked down at her. From the rise in the front of his jeans, she knew he wasn't talking about the print.

She cleared her throat and went back to looking at the walls, her pulse picking up, her middle was growing moist, yeah she needed to hang the damn print and get the hell out of this man's house!

"Well, do you conduct business in this office or just work in it?" she asked, trying to ignore all the signals he was putting out and her own damn hormones at the same time.

Jazz propped the print against the wall carefully before moving even closer to Tayana.

"No, I usually don't conduct business here but *we* sure as hell could put in some work here," he whispered in her ear. He bit the tip of her ear and began to lightly drag his fingertips up her arms, leaving a trail of chill bumps where his fingertips touched.

Tayana turned so her whole body was facing him, but before she could utter a word, Jazz backed her up against the wall and forced his tongue in her mouth. His hands held her in place by her hips while he was grinding his erection against her.

Tayana's hands found their way into the opening of his shirt and began moving all over his muscular chest. When her thumb skated across his nipple, he hissed and lightly captured her bottom lip between his teeth.

His hands moved from her hips and under her blouse, lightly dragging across her stomach causing more chill bumps to appear.

"Tayana," he whispered in her ear as his hands moved higher and hers moved lower.

Hearing him use her actual name added fuel to the flames rolling through her body. Her small hand cupped and rubbed his erection through his jeans.

He was kissing her softly on her neck, his hands made quick work of unsnapping her bra and were now holding her breasts, thumbs teasing her nipples.

Tayana leaned forward and began placing soft kisses on his bare chest, she allowed her tongue to drag across one nipple then the other. Her hand was still caressing his erection through his jeans.

Jazz pulled her shirt over her head, draped it over his high back desk chair and picked her up off her feet kissing her again. She wrapped her legs around his waist kissing him back with enthusiasm. She grabbed both sides of his head and pushed her tongue deeper into his mouth.

He moaned, his tongue moving deeper inside of Tayana's welcoming mouth as he turned and carried her out of the office, through the great room before climbing up his dark mahogany staircase.

When they reached his room, he slid her down his body and back on her feet. Dropping to his knees, he reached under her pant leg and touched her ankle holster looking up at her.

"I'm going to ask you one last time, do you trust me, Tayana? If you don't know what I'm about by now then there is no hope for us and this thing between us is over, right here, right now," he told her, his eyes flashed in the darkened room as he continued to look up at her.

Tayana's heart was already beating fast, it picked up even faster as she looked down at him. This was it, she needed to make a choice about Jazz and about their relationship once and for all, if she wanted this thing between them to continue, she needed to let go of control and let her heart lead her. She fought the urge to move her ankle out of his grasp which seemed natural to her and closed her eyes, lifting up a silent prayer and hoping she wouldn't live to regret her next move.

"Yes, Jazz, I trust you," she answered softly, opening her eyes. He stared up at her as he took off her holster and gun, aiming it towards the wall and placed it on the bedside table closest to where they were standing. The reassuring look he gave her told her, Mary Jane was just a reach away.

Jazz stayed on his knees and removed her stilettos. When he reached up to unfasten her slacks, he looked up at her again. "Still good?"

He didn't wait for her to answer this time before unfastening and helping her out of her slacks and draping them on the chair behind him. He hooked his fingers in the elastic resting on her waist and slowly dragged the silk and lace material down her legs, dropping her thong on the floor behind him.

"Let me ask you something, Tayana, don't you ever get tired of being in complete control all the time? Don't you wish sometimes you could just let someone else take control and take care of you?" he asked her, standing to his full height and kissing her on the neck again.

"What does it matter, Jazz? Why are you asking me that, especially now?" Tayana asked softly, biting her bottom lip and pulling her arms out of the straps of her unfastened bra and dropping it down in front of him.

"Because right now is when I want to know. I realize you are used to being in charge but when it's just the two of us, like we are now, I'm in charge, can you get with that, Tayana?" Jazz asked her looking at her like he was going to devour her at any moment.

Her body was covered in chill bumps, her pussy begged for attention and wet her inner thighs, perfuming the air with her scent of arousal, her clit pulsated and swelled screaming for his touch. Shit, little did he know he was already in control but still she protested.

"In charge how, Jazz?" she asked, her eyes narrowing at him even as her hormones screamed for her to shut the hell up so he could finish what he started.

Jazz bit his bottom lip and moved in closer to her. "Meaning, when we are in this room, you will do what I say without question. If you disobey me or upset me then there will be consequences," he said, coming forward and kissing her softly on the lips.

Tayana's normal response would be to tell Jazz he could go straight to Hell and leave, however, something about letting go and submitting to Jazz intrigued her and the consequences he mentioned, well, let's just say she was curious as hell to find out what they might be.

"So what do you say, Tayana? Are you willing to do this for me?" Jazz asked her while massaging her already hardened nipple with the palm of his hand.

Tayana closed her eyes and moaned at the sensations

moving through her body. When she didn't immediately answer Jazz pinched her nipple hard.

"Answer me, Tayana," he commanded, pinching harder before biting her on the neck.

Tayana's middle poured wetness down her thighs immediately. Shit, that felt good! "Yes, Jazz. Yes, I am willing to give you control when it's just the two of us."

A truly wicked grin spread across his face when she opened her eyes and looked up at him. "Excellent. Let's begin," he said, kneeling back down. "First things first, Tayana, I don't like being ignored or repeating myself. When I tell you to do something, in private and in public settings, you do it. If you don't, you will be punished," he warned and reached for her shoes and helped her put them back on.

The clothes whore in her appreciated the move, her black and white, crystal encrusted Alexander McQueen's were a work of art all on their own.

He leaned forward, spread her pussy lips and placed a soft kiss on her clit before standing back up in front of her, hard as steel, licking his lips again slowly.

"Undress me," he commanded, dropping his hands to his sides.

Tayana covered the small distance between them and unbuttoned the three remaining buttons on his shirt before reaching up and pushing it off of his broad shoulders, letting it drop at his feet. The minute it touched the ground, Jazz delivered a stinging smack to her ass.

"Now I know you know better than that," he growled, narrowing his eyes at her.

"Ouch! Dammit that hurt, Jazz!" She fussed trying to ignore how good it really felt.

He smacked her on her ass again. "Quiet, Tayana and get the shirt off the floor before I really get upset," he warned her, his light eyes were getting darker and looked almost menacing. What the fuck had she just signed up for?

She picked up his shirt, carefully shook it out, and walked slowly over to drape it on the back of the same chair where her slacks rested. She then walked back to Jazz.

"Never make that mistake again," he told her, as he grabbed her arm, pulled her tight to his side with his arm looped around her waist before a series of smacks rained down on her backside causing her to moan involuntarily as more of her nectar poured down her thighs, she could see the wetness shining in the pale light that shined through his bedroom window. "Now, the pants," he instructed watching her every move.

Tayana ran her hands down his bare chest slowly, her entire body tingled as she reached his jeans and unbuttoned them, slipping them down his hips along with his underwear.

She pushed him back on the bed before dropping to her knees, and taking off his loafers. After placing them next to the bed, she pulled his jeans and underwear completely off.

"Kiss it," he demanded after she put his pants on the back of the chair next to his shirt and her slacks. Something about this more demanding side of Jazz had her pulse racing, making her even more aroused than she was before.

His erection stood proudly reaching a little past his belly button. Tayana came up and placed one knee on the bed, leaned forward and ran her tongue from the bottom of his balls to the tip of his shaft, sucking the head, then stood back up. His dick jumped enthusiastically as he moaned, letting his head fall back on the bed.

"Ready to die, Jazz?" Tayana whispered. His body jerked in alarm. She was standing right next to the bedside table and Mary Jane.

Chapter 7

Tayana chuckled softly when she saw his body jerk in surprise. "Relax, baby, it's not what you think," she said softly looking down at him. She moved her hands slowly up and down her body, swaying from side to side to the soft, sexy music playing from somewhere in the room. *"Sweet Baby"* by Gerald Albright seduced her music loving ears as she seduced Jazz.

Jazz came up on his elbows, his eyes followed her hands as they roamed all over her body, her hands cupped her full breasts and skated across her erect nipples, she moved her hands down her taut stomach and ran her finger down her wet slit, causing her oversensitive clit to send waves of want ricocheting through her. She smiled seductively as she watched him grow even harder while watching her move.

When she saw she had him completely relaxed again and under her spell, Tayana slowly crawled up his body until she was face to face with him. She took her time and kissed each eye, his nose, his goatee, before lightly kissing his lips. *"La petite mort,"* she whispered, spreading her legs and straddling his lap, his rock-hard dick resting between her wet pussy lips.

The minute her tongue parted his lips he rolled over pinning her beneath him, deeply kissing her while moving between her legs.

"I'm in charge, remember?" he ground out, glaring down at her. That little comment of hers about him being ready to die had him heated, her little dance had him horny as hell! Yeah she was going to pay for both, he thought to himself while forcing his tongue as deep as it would go inside her mouth.

After a few minutes of treating her to his searing kisses, Jazz reluctantly pulled his lips from hers and his lips and tongue began their journey down her body. He stopped at her breasts, sucking each one in turn, his finger teased her clit before sliding deep into her wet center.

Tayana moaned and arched off the bed, her hips moving with his fingers. Jazz placed a second finger inside of her and massaged her clit with his thumb.

"Jazz... Damn..." Tayana moaned as he sucked harder on her breasts, his teeth teased and bit her nipples lightly at first then harder causing her to grow even wetter and arch off the bed to meet his thrusting fingers.

When he felt her begin to tighten, he released her breast and moved further down her body. He took her legs and placed them on his shoulders and brought his mouth to her most sacred treasure by guiding her to him by her hips. He ran his tongue down her center tasting her love honey before teasing her clit with his tongue until it stood up so tall it peeked from between her swollen lips as if it was looking for him. Jazz fastened his warm mouth around it and sucked it eagerly, causing Tayana to writhe and squirm as she tightly gripped the sheets underneath her.

Tayana closed her eyes and bit her bottom lip as Jazz continued to feast on her. When she felt her orgasm building, she tried to move back from his mouth. Jazz drove his tongue deep inside of her box, moving it from side to side touching every inch of her innermost secrets.

"Oh fuck! Jazz, oh fuck!" She chanted as she started her descent into bliss, he quickly moved his mouth away from her quivering box and lowered her hips on the bed. Tayana reached out, grabbing the back of his head trying to push him forward to continue. He refused to allow her to move his head back between her legs causing her to moan in frustration. "Jazz, please."

Jazz kissed her on her inner thighs, blew lightly on her pubic hair, even lightly brushed his thumb across her clit but refused to give her exactly what he knew she wanted.

Tayana gripped the sheets tightly as she shivered with need, she arched her back and moved her hips to combat the battle going on inside her body, he could tell she was on the brink of coming and wanted him to take her there and he would, but in his time not hers.

"You will learn, Tayana. Like I said a few minutes ago, I am in charge, so that slick mouth of yours will continuously get your ass in trouble here," he informed her while running his tongue up her thigh. He grinned evilly as he heard her pitiful moan as she began to squirm for him to continue. "Do you want me to help you come, Tayana?" he asked with his lips brushing lightly against her second set of lips.

"Yes, Jazz, please." She moaned again and arched her back to press her mound against his lips, he moved his head away immediately.

"Not so fast beautiful one, do you even have any idea why you're being punished?" Jazz tsked, kissing her on her lower abdomen right above her pelvic bone while pressing her hips down to make her relax on the bed.

"Jazz, please! I don't know and I don't honestly care, please stop doing me like this," Tayana whined, kicking her feet in frustration.

Jazz shook his head sadly and sighed. "There goes that mouth, and wrong answer, Tayana," he taunted, blowing softly in her pubic hairs. "Now, I'm going to ask you again, do you have any idea why you're being punished?" he asked, using his tongue to flick her clit.

"Ugh! I don't know! I don't know! I don't know! Jazz, please don't do this to me!" she cried out, moving her hips off the bed again.

Jazz pressed her hips down on the bed and held her in place, chuckling a little. "Stubborn ass woman, think hard, Tayana," he coaxed, as she continued to squirm underneath him, barely containing the devilish smile tugging at his face.

Finally, he had her where he wanted her and he was loving every minute of it. The minute she agreed to let him take control in the bedroom, he knew it was time for a little payback. He leaned forward and flicked her clit with his tongue before sucking on it for a split second and moving away again.

Her immediate response flooded the bed sheets below her, he couldn't resist moving forward again and sucking the moisture from her pubic hairs.

"Damn, Tayana you taste so fucking good! Too bad I'm going to have to stop because you insist on being so fucking stubborn," he taunted huskily, sitting up on his knees, using the palm of his hand he pressed down on her abdomen to still her swaying hips as she moaned and whined.

Her entire body was shiny with sweat, her titties moved from side to side invitingly as she panted and breathed heavily, he assumed she was on the brink of sexual madness the way she babbled and threw her head from side to side with her eyes closed tight.

"Jazz, I don't know what I did but whatever it is I didn't mean to do it or upset you, I can't take this anymore! I can't take it! Jazz please, I need you!" she cried out, her body writhing beneath his hand.

Jazz slowly pushed his middle finger into her moist channel and began to move it in and out painfully slow. He could feel her walls begin to move and constrict around his finger, he pushed a second finger inside of her creamy wetness and pushed his fingers in as deep as they would go.

"Need me for what? Tell me what you need me to do, Tayana. You know I long to make you happy, baby," he teased, still moving his fingers inside of her.

"I need you to kiss my lips, eat my pussy, finger me, fuck me, I don't really care I just need you in any way I can get you!" Tayana ground out with her teeth clenched as she fought against his strong hand that had her pinned to the bed.

"You know, normally, I would make you suffer more because you still haven't told me the actual reason you're being punished, and while your sweet suffering is music to my ears, Imma let you off easy because I feel like I'm about to fucking burst!" Jazz removed his fingers, quickly grabbed a condom from his bedside table and rolled it on before grabbing her by the hips and pushing his dick inside of her deep and hard.

"Oh my *fucking God, yes*!" Tayana screamed out, throwing her arms around Jazz's neck as he pumped in and out of her like a fucking savage. Happy tears sprang from her eyes and rolled down her face. Finally! Fucking finally! She'd felt like she was going to lose her ever-loving mind if he didn't touch her. She felt his balls slapping against her ass and he wreaked havoc on her pussy.

"Damn, Tayana, you feel even better than you taste." Jazz moaned as he continued to move hard and fast in and out of her dripping wet opening. He slid his hands under her ass and brought her up to meet his every thrust.

"Oh my God! Jazz, you're so deep." Tayana moaned, feeling his manly thrusts deep into her lower abdomen. She grabbed his muscular arms and held on tight, Jazz was working the hell out of her pussy!

The way he was pounding inside of her she was sure, that long after they both came and were more than satisfied, she would still remember how deep inside of her he was with every step she took for days.

Jazz slowed down to kiss her deeply again. "Yeah, I know I am, that's what your ass gets for making me wait so fucking long," he snapped and sped up even more, biting her bottom lip before he came up on his hands, slamming into her and moving his hips from side to side hitting every inch of her channel.

Tayana grabbed his head, bringing his mouth back to hers and forcing her tongue deep inside his mouth. When she began to suck on his tongue, his tempo increased, even more, his balls slapped against her ass sending her even further over the edge of bliss and closer to her chasm of orgasmic fulfillment.

She felt the veins of his dick grow and throb against her walls, she worked her vaginal muscles and contracted and squeezed to make sure she took him over the edge right along with her.

Jazz came up on his knees and gripped her thighs tightly, drilling into her drenched middle, taking back control of their lust fest and personally escorting her to her very own pleasurable hell.

The first whispers of orgasm radiated in her throbbing center and surged deep inside of her before sending shockwaves through her entire body, outward like a mushroom cloud of desire. She threw her head back and screamed loud enough to wake the dead.

"Jazz! Goddamn, baby! Goddamn! Yes! Baby! Yes! I'm coming! I'm coming! I'm fucking coming! Oh God, yes!" Tayana cried out at the top of her lungs, shockwaves and chills of euphoria rolling through her causing her to shiver and shake even more as Jazz continued to stroke her deeper and deeper.

Jazz still had a death grip on her thighs doing damage to her middle as her pleasure took her higher and higher, taking her breath away.

Jazz soon followed Tayana over the edge and threw his head back with a loud groan. "Fuck, Tayana! Fuck!" he roared, clenching his jaw tight, still pounding away on her little lady.

The force at which his orgasm left his body was testing the durability of the latex barrier between them. "Tayana! Shit! Baby, damn!" he shouted, biting the inside of her ankle as he shivered and shook.

When he finished emptying his load into the condom, he pulled out and gently took her legs off of his shoulders and moved forward until his head was resting on her chest, his body still between her legs.

Aftershocks were still making Tayana's body jerk, she was bathed in sweat, her breathing still heavy and labored like after a good workout. Jazz pulled her into his arms and held her tight until her body stilled underneath him.

"Turn over," he whispered when she was completely still. Getting up on his knees, he reached down and helped her up. Tayana repositioned herself and lay on her stomach with her eyes closed. Jazz leaned over her and softly blew down her back, giving her even more chills than before.

Another orgasm immediately clawed its way up her spine. "Shit! Shit! Shit!" Tayana screamed as her orgasm rocked her from the inside out, she bit down on the sheet beneath her riding the waves of desire once again.

Jazz lay next to her and watched her in the throes of passion, a small sexy grin on his face, "Tayana, you are so beautiful, especially right now," he whispered as she came back to him.

Tayana turned her head facing him. Her body was too heavy for any other movement at the moment. "Damn, Jazz, that was amazing, you are amazing."

He dragged his hand lazily down her spine. "My pleasure, but you know you had something coming for that shit you said."

Tayana lifted her head frowning. "What shit?" she asked, confused and still recovering from her second orgasm.

"That 'are you ready to die shit'!" He smacked her hard on the ass. "I didn't appreciate it in the least."

Tayana yelped before pulling herself up on her elbows, damn she loved it when he did that! "It was a play on words carried over from the night on the beach. I told you I would tell you when it was time to die, remember?" Tayana explained lifting her head and looking at him.

Jazz stared up at the ceiling for a moment, Tayana assumed probably going through his mental rolodex to remember the night on the beach.

"Okay, then what was that other shit you whispered, did you cast a spell or curse on me, woman?" he asked, pulling off the condom, leaning over and dropping it in the trash can beside the table next to the bed.

Tayana stared at him, her face expressionless refusing to answer his question. She liked the reaction ignoring him got her.

"Boss Lady, what did you say?" he asked, looking serious. "Don't play with me, I don't think you're ready for what I will really do to your ass if you do," he warned, smacking her on the ass again, twice this time.

Tayana let a small smile play on her face as she realized Jazz called her 'Boss Lady' when he was annoyed or truly pissed at her and 'Tayana' when he wanted her or was feeling some other strong emotion about her.

"*La petite mort* is French for 'The little death'," she finally told him, her ass was stinging from the smacks he delivered and she wasn't ready for another one just yet.

Jazz's eyebrow arched, looking like he was getting upset. "So you did wish death on me?"

Tayana reached over and ran her finger across his lips. "No, baby, it means to have an orgasm."

Jazz looked over at her confused. "Are you fucking with me, Tayana?"

Tayana pushed him on his back and straddled his hips. "What do you think, Jazz? Should I fuck with you?" she asked before leaning forward to kiss him.

His 'friend' immediately began to wake back up. He grabbed her hips to move her to the tip of his growing erection and she pushed his hands off her.

"No, Jazz, you think I'm fucking with you, so let me fuck with you," Tayana teased, leaning forward pinning his hands to the bed with her own. Her breasts brushed against his bare chest causing her nipples to harden again and her to moan.

She kissed his lips briefly before moving slowly down his body, dragging her tongue across his soft skin along the way. When she was face to face with his rock-hard dick, she paused. He flexed and made it jump. She chuckled, before running her tongue over the tip and then swallowing his shaft until it hit the back of her throat.

"Damn, Tayana!" he whispered fiercely, placing his hand on the back of her head. He began to thrust into her mouth.

Tayana moved his hand and let his erection drop from her mouth.

When he was still again, she captured him in her mouth once more. She pulled back to the tip, sucked on his helmet, and flicked her tongue in his hole before taking him even deeper into her mouth, he could feel her bottom lip brushing against the top of his scrotum as she sucked him off.

"Fuck!" he hissed, grabbing the sheets and beginning to grind against her mouth again. Again Tayana slowly and deliberately removed him from her mouth.

"Tayana, are you fucking kidding me?" he screamed, his toes curling.

Tayana chuckled again and crawled back up his body and slowly lowered herself onto his erection.

Jazz arched his back and grabbed her hips to push himself deeper inside her. She pushed his hands off her and came up until just the very tip of his erection was parting her pussy lips.

Jazz's eyes darkened, throwing venom at her, catching on to what was going on. "Boss Lady, I swear to God if you don't stop fucking with me..." he growled through gritted teeth looking like he was going to tear her apart.

She slid down his shaft and worked her hips until he was in as deep as he could go. She didn't move, she just relished the feeling and ran her hands all over his chest.

Jazz looked pissed off but also curious, he seemed willing to allow her to finish her little game. He bit his bottom lip and fought the urge to move or touch her. He closed his eyes, his face contorted as if he was in pain, husky whispers of both threats and praise began to fall from his mouth.

His hands pulled the sheets from the mattress as he waited for her to move. "Boss Lady, please baby, Tayana, damn! You are killing me!" he ground out, opening his eyes and drawing her in with a sexy ass glare.

A small devious smile spread across Tayana's face as she

began to move. She came off her knees and planted her feet on the bed and did squats and Kegels up and down Jazz's swollen erection.

He fought to remain still and let her play. He cussed, he moaned, he gripped the sheets even tighter until they were wound up tight around each of his hands, his toes curled, his muscles were flexed and taut as she milked the hell out of his dick with her pussy muscles.

When she felt the veins of his dick pulsating faster, she leaned forward and whispered, "Touch me."

Jazz's eyes, which had been squinted and closed tight in sweet anguish, opened to glare at her as he took her by the hips and slammed her down on his erection over and over again. Damn, it felt good to be inside of her and before she was ready for it she felt her walls tightening, she milked him some more begging him to join her.

He threw his head back and roared her name as he emptied inside of her, her walls quivering with her own orgasm held him tight until his last thrust.

"Holy Shit!" Jazz fell back hard on his pillows, panting to catch his breath.

"*La petite mort,*" Tayana whispered softly, laying her head on his chest. "It was better to show you than try to explain it." His semi-hard dick still rested inside of her.

"Shit, you got anything else you want to show me? You are one hell of a teacher," Jazz asked, looking down at her, eyes getting heavy.

"I sincerely doubt you could handle another lesson tonight," Tayana murmured, placing a soft kiss on his chest.

"Not at the moment, but give me a few hours and I will be ready." He wrapped his arms around her as his eyes closed.

"Oh, no. I have to drive home at some point tonight and there's no time like the present, while I can still walk." Tayana moved to get up and out of his arms when his eyes popped open.

"Not happening. Your little pretty ass is staying right here tonight, Boss Lady," he told her matter of factly holding her tight in the circle of his arms.

"Jazz, come on, stop playing. I need to go home!" Tayana began to struggle when he brought his mouth to hers and kissed her softly.

"All you need to do right now is listen to your man, Tayana, and I say you're staying here with me. You're staying here, case closed," he told her and started kissing her again.

What little fight she had left, evaporated. Besides, she was coming to realize she really liked it when he took charge like that. She allowed herself to be lulled to sleep by the low playing music in his room, Jazz's breathing and heartbeat.

Tayana's first ever walk of shame felt so shameful and she wasn't even out of the damn car yet! She stayed at Jazz's place for two days, conducting business over the phone and never did hang the damn print. He gave her a tour of sorts of his house, she saw several rooms in fact, well the ceilings anyway.

She hated to admit it, but he had her nose open and she was beyond sprung! Jazz's ass made sure of that fact quite well.

Her entire body was humming happily beneath the soreness she felt all over. Jazz had most definitely left his mark on every inch of her, she was already missing all of him like crazy but knew they had to break the spell sometime.

Now all she wanted to do was go up to her room and sleep for the rest of the day and start fresh in the morning. She knew her ladies were never going to let her hear the end of this shit but the sexathon Jazz threw on her ass was worth the headache!

She pulled into her driveway and swore silently to herself as she pulled up to the front of her house. All of her ladies' cars were parked outside at 6 a.m.

"Shit! Shit! Shit!" she mumbled, hitting her steering wheel. Bruise was leaning on her black town car, arms folded with a smirk.

"Who are you again?" he teased, as she stepped out of the Land Rover.

Tayana cut her eyes in his direction before moving towards the house.

"Hey, all joking aside, was that what you were wearing when you left the other day from Essie's?" Bruise asked, his smile tugging at the corners of his mouth.

Tayana blushed deeply and sighed. "No it isn't, B. Now drop the subject please," she ordered softly, rushing past him and up the porch steps towards the house and the inquisition she knew was about to go down.

The truth was she had no idea where her clothes were. She spent the last two days in one of Jazz's button downs, well when she actually had on clothes at all, even her underwear came up missing!

"You look nice, nonetheless, Whisper, all shiny and shit!" Bruise chuckled as she stopped at the top of the porch stairs to shoot him an evil glare and entered the house.

"Not funny, B!" she called over her shoulder and closed the door behind her.

Surprised she wasn't ambushed at the door, she slipped off her new Manolo's and rushed to her office to drop off her briefcase. As soon as she hit the door, all her ladies jumped up and applauded.

"Whoo Whoo, Jazz is the man, look at her all glowing and

shit! Oh, and check out the outfit that screams, 'Jazz Jones'!" Yolan cheered.

She looked down at her black pants and cream-colored blouse with thin black stripes. He insisted on buying it for her; the lingerie she wore underneath was from him too. He felt guilty that her clothes had disappeared.

Tayana moved and took her seat at the head of the table silently and slowly. "So, ladies, how's business?" she asked, looking out at each of them in turn.

They all exchanged looks ranging from confusion to concern before Joy sat up, clearing her throat. "Business is flowing smoothly as usual, Whisper, no problems or issues."

A slow smile crept across Tayana's face. "That's good to hear because I am tired and sore as hell!" Tayana folded her arms on the table and dropped her head on them.

All the ladies cheered and started all talking at once.

"Whisper, the gentleman with the $25,000 frame is up front demanding to speak with you, he looks upset." Sasha rushed into her office two weeks later looking concerned.

She and Jazz had spent every free moment they could together. It had been four days since their last date and she was in need of some Jazz Jones sexual healing!

"Well, send him back." Tayana's heartbeat immediately picked up as it did every time she saw or even thought about Jazz.

She bit the inside of her cheek and fought the urge to smile her flirty smile when Sasha led him back to her office. His light gray suit made him look edible.

Tayana stood and moved from behind her desk smiling her most professional smile in spite of the fact he was wearing her thighs like earmuffs the last time she saw him.

"Good afternoon, Mr. Jones. How can I be of assistance?" Tayana extended her hand for him to shake.

He shook her hand in return staring at her, his erection already beginning to tent his pants, thank God his back was to Sasha so she couldn't see it.

"I am sorry for just dropping in like this but I wanted to discuss the possibility of purchasing more prints and having you frame them. I understand there are three more in the 'Lock & Key' series," Jazz said, watching Sasha head back to the showroom.

"Yes, there are the two with the lovers down on one knee individually, 'Lock and Key Male' and 'Lock and Key Female' and the final in the series 'Lock and Key United' the lovers are embracing with the key finally inside the lock," she told him in her most professional voice, walking past him to close and lock the door to her office.

He moved all the way into her office and stood in front of her desk. He watched her walk back to her desk before looking around at the concrete walls of her office.

"How soundproof is this office?" Jazz grabbed her to him, pushing his tongue into her mouth, kissing her until she was dizzy.

Tayana grabbed the desk to steady herself still facing him when he let her go. "Completely," she whispered, pulling her black pencil skirt up and over her hips, exposing one of the sexy sets he sent her recently. She stood before him showing off her black lace thong, garter, and thigh-high silk stockings.

"Damn, I'm a lucky man," Jazz murmured, shaking his head as he dropped to his knees. He playfully nipped at her pubic hairs through the lace before removing her thong and burying his face deep between her legs.

"And I am a lucky woman, damn, Jazz!" Tayana moaned through clenched teeth. He grabbed her and sat her down on the edge of her desk reclaiming his spot between her legs with his mouth.

He feasted on her, sucking her clit, and sucking on her juices as they poured out of her. Tayana lay back on her desk and spread her legs wider giving Jazz better access to her center. His mouth and tongue dived even deeper; she grabbed him by the back of his head and rode his face like a champ. Fuck, she loved how free she felt with Jazz!

Way too soon, she felt the orgasm moving up her spine. Jazz stopped tasting her and unzipped his pants freeing his erection. Picking Tayana up, he positioned her right over his erection and used her hips to move her up and down, standing in the middle of her office.

Her breasts slipped out of her half-cup bra, the friction of the silk of her blouse on her nipples caused them to stand up stiff and erect, hoping they were next in line for his pleasure giving mouth. Jazz kissed her mouth, her neck, and back to her mouth again.

He lowered her to the mink throw on her office floor and pushed her blouse up and quickly captured a breast in his mouth still moving deep inside of her.

Tayana's moans echoed through her office. Her legs were locked around Jazz's waist; her hands gripped his ass, pushing him deeper inside of her. When he was as deep as he could get inside of her she moved and swiveled her hips beneath him rising to meet his thrusts.

"Goddamn, Tayana! Shit, baby, shit! This pussy is so fucking good!"

He clenched his teeth as he felt her begin to come; just as she began to tighten he began to come, biting her on the shoulder. They stayed stuck together as the waves of orgasm took them to another level in the middle of her office.

"I'm sorry about your throw," Jazz apologized, when he pulled out some of his load landed on her throw rug. He was sitting across from her while she was sitting behind her desk trying to catch her breath.

Tayana's hair was now down, her natural wave pattern falling over her shoulders, Jazz had fucked her bun loose. She looked content and well-fucked as she searched the internet for the other two prints in the size he wanted them in.

"I'm sorry about your slacks," Tayana countered, looking down at his crotch, his slacks were hopelessly wrinkled, the knees were deeply creased from kneeling before her.

Jazz pulled her lace thong from his suit jacket pocket and held it to his nose, inhaling deeply. "It was so worth it, damn your pussy smells amazing," he said grinning at her wickedly.

Tayana's mouth dropped open in surprise. "You are so fucking nasty, Jazz!" she said, shaking her head and ordering the prints.

"Only around your sexy ass." He chuckled and slipped her thong back into his pocket.

"Um, hello? I need those back." Tayana sat back, holding her hand out, crossing her legs.

Jazz licked his lips, sitting back in his seat. "No, you don't. Let Bruise know I'm picking you up after you close up tonight."

Tayana's pussy jumped in anticipation. "How do you know I don't have plans tonight?" she asked. Hell, she couldn't be so damn easy all of the damn time! She fought against her smile and lost.

"Do you have plans tonight, Tayana?" he asked, giving her a maddening look.

She stared over at him taking in his sexy-ass, freshly-fucked look.

"Hmm, as a matter of fact I do. Does riding your face

until the sun comes up count as plans?" Tayana asked uncrossing her legs, giving him a beaver shot.

Jazz licked his lips, looking like he was savoring the taste of something delicious, and smiled while standing up. "That's what's up. How long do you think it will be before those other three prints are ready?"

"Two to three weeks depending on how long it takes to get the wood for the frame in." Tayana's gaze landed on his wrinkled crotch. "Do you have any more meetings today?" she asked, shaking her head.

He came behind her desk and leaned in to kiss her, his hands on the armrests of her chair. "Just one, but don't worry. Chomps is nowhere near as beautiful as you are."

Tayana kissed him back and pushed his head away from her neck. "Just be sure to wear your jacket. Can't have people thinking a clothes whore like you is falling off, now can we?" she teased.

"You're one to talk, do you think that wet spot will come out of the back of your skirt?" he asked, standing back up and sauntering over to the door. "It's always a business doing pleasure with you, Tayana. Please have Sasha send me an invoice for my prints once you know the price."

He winked and left her office.

Tayana closed her eyes and sighed contently before watching Jazz leave on the security cameras. His driver opened the door for him, he put on his sunglasses and slipped in the back seat of his custom Bugatti.

His security pulled away from the curb with their windows down, amateurs, their carelessness really set her teeth on edge.

Her private cellphone vibrated on her desk. *I miss you already. See you tonight* was the text message from Jazz.

Tayana sat staring at the message, grinning like a fool for about two minutes, before she forced herself to close the message and lock her phone.

Chapter 8

"Whisper, we have a new potential client for fabric cleaning. Thing is, he wants to meet with you before we proceed. Looks like he has some interest in the discoveries from the Motherland as well," Monet reported in code when Tayana answered her phone a few nights later.

Jazz's hand was moving up her leg, she stilled it. Jazz nodded, taking the hint she was talking business and climbed off the bed wearing jeans, unfastened with no underwear underneath, and to Tayana he looked like her greatest temptation personified.

"Dinner, meet me in the kitchen in ten minutes," he ordered, whispering in her ear, "Don't make me come back up here, Whisper, you promised me a home cooked meal tonight and as much as I love trying to, I can't live on coochie alone." He threw her a sexy smile and wink before leaving her to handle business.

"Interesting," Tayana said to Monet, shaking her head at Jazz in surprise at his comment as he left the room, the stuff that came tumbling out of his damn mouth sometimes! "Well, set up a meeting and let me know when it is. Anything I need to know about him or his people?" she asked refocusing on Monet and the phone call.

Monet sighed. "New to the area, Khyrs and Jaidyn are working on that now, I won't schedule the meeting until we hear back from them," she answered.

"Okay sounds good, anything else?" Tayana asked, standing up to go join Jazz in the kitchen, ten minutes meant eight minutes in Jazz speak and her ass was already sore from mouthing off earlier.

"Yeah, just one more thing," Monet answered.

Tayana thought about his huge hands making contact with her backside and began to squirm a little bit, she hoped she could handle the rest of Monet's call quickly, she was starving for food and for Jazz as dessert. She just couldn't get enough of the damn man.

"Yes?" she asked patiently, standing up and moving towards the stairs in the hallway.

"Are you even letting the poor man up for air, Whisper? I mean the last thing you need is a murder case!" Monet teased, cackling into the phone.

"Fuck you, Mo!" Tayana ended the call and descended the staircase heading for the kitchen.

"Everything okay?" Jazz asked, handing her a glass of white wine when she walked in.

"Yeah, you know how it is, business, business and more business but my ladies are the best, so it's all good," she told him sipping the wine.

He leaned on the counter sipping his own glass of wine, watching her as she went to the fridge and grabbed the lamb chops she had been marinating overnight. He was still looking at her deep in thought.

"What's up, Jazz? Where you at?" she asked, turning on the grill attached to his stove to heat it up before looking at him.

She was at his place so much now, she knew his kitchen almost as good as she knew her own. Even with Ms. Lanie living with her and cooking most of her meals, she still sometimes had the urge to cook for herself and recently she learned she really loved cooking for Jazz.

"I'm just wondering. If you weren't doing what you do, Whisper what would you have wanted to do?" he asked her, still watching her thoughtfully.

She frowned and shrugged, before turning back towards the stove. "What? What kind of question is that, Jazz?" She pulled out a pair of tongs and laid the three minty smelling chops onto the now hot grill surface.

Jazz reached out and turned her around so she was facing him again. "I'm serious, Tayana, answer me," he ordered, reaching behind her and turning the grill down to low now that it was hot.

"Your mind, Jazz, I swear." Tayana sighed and clicked the tongs she was holding in her hand. "I honestly have no idea, Jazz, but it's a moot point anyway, this is the business I'm in so it is what it is. Besides, technically I am doing what I wanted to do with my life, running Essie's," she answered and walked over to grab a pot and fill it with hot water for the couscous she was making to go with the lamb.

He watched her silently as she moved around the kitchen putting together their dinner. She felt his eyes on her and refused to turn around, what the hell was wrong with him asking her something like that? As if she had a fucking choice at this point, this was the only life she knew, it was damn near in her DNA, his, too, for that matter.

"Tayana, be honest with me. Sometimes when I look at you, I can see something working in that beautiful mind of yours, tell me I'm wrong," he said, reaching for her once she put all of their food on, grabbed her wineglass off the counter and faced him.

"Jazz, if you're asking me if I regret the line of work I'm in, the answer is no, I don't. This is who I am, what I was born into and, despite my father trying to push me out, I'm damn good at it. Just look at the empire my ladies and I have built. We are killing the game on our terms. That being said, sometimes I have to admit it's exhausting being on alert and on guard at times. Just look at us and how long it took for me to let you in. Neither of us had much of a choice, Jazz, but here we are and I, for one, am okay with it," Tayana admitted, really tripping that he knew her so well already.

Sometimes she thought about phasing them out of the illegal parts of the business and building up the legitimate ones sooner, rather than later, but right now it just wasn't an option.

"What about you, Jazz? If you weren't Jazz Jones of HTown, what profession would you have chosen?" Tayana moved back to the fridge to grab the ingredients for their salad and pulled out a wooden bowl to put it in.

"Like you, I honestly don't know. My business, this business is all I know and I have to agree with you I'm damn good at what I do but the older I get, the more I have to wonder if this is the legacy I would want to leave for our family," he told her, kissing her on the forehead and pouring her more wine.

Tayana almost sliced off the tip of her finger, looking at Jazz, did he just say, 'Their family'? What the what! She cleared her throat and finished cutting the cucumber in front of her into thin slices choosing to ignore his last statement.

"Where is all of this coming from, Jazz?" she asked, moving the green pepper closer to chop it too.

"Tayana, don't act like you didn't hear what I said, you

know I really hate when you do that." He walked over and put his finger under her chin forcing her to look up at him.

"And you know I hate it when you play word games with me, Jazz, say what you mean and mean what you say. What is all of this about? Real talk. We are just getting to know each other and you're talking about us having a family together, what's up? I mean for real, for real." She laid the knife down on the cutting board, staring deep into his eyes trying to understand what she saw there.

The muscle in his jaw jumped when he clenched his teeth and he let his hand drop from her face, then turned to take the lamb chops off the grill before they were overcooked. Tayana watched him nervously, he still had his back to her as he grabbed two plates out of one of the upper cabinets and put the lamb chops on them, two on his plate and one on hers.

She made herself turn around, and silently made quick work of the vegetables for their salad, tossing them all in the wooden bowl when she was finished. Her hands shook as she rinsed off the knife and cutting board and put them in the dishwasher, his silence scared her more than the 'their family' comment.

Was he saying or about to say what she thought he was and was she ready to hear it?

Tayana sighed and set the salad on the table, she turned to grab the salad bowls and ran into Jazz who had just brought the plates with lamb and couscous to the table as well.

"Sorry, I was just about to grab the—" He stopped her mid-sentence, grabbed her and kissed her deeply. There was so much more passion behind the kiss than usual and it had Tayana weak in the knees by the time he let her go.

"I love you, Tayana. I'm in love with you, Boss Lady," Jazz admitted, looking down at her, still holding her tight.

She could see the look of relief as it spread across his face just as she felt her mind shift into panic mode, he was in love with her? Shit and double shit!

His declaration of love had her thinking about how she felt, really felt about him. Yeah she loved spending all of her free time with him, looked forward to his calls and text messages, thought about him constantly, and hadn't stopped smiling or humming love songs since she decided to trust him, but was that love? Like geeked up true love or was it just infatuation because of the newness of them?

"Relax, Tayana, I know how your mind works and in this instance I'm glad it does work that way. If it makes you feel any better I have no fucking idea what it means for us in this moment, but I do know I see you as my wife and the mother of my children at some point in our lives. So you've got time to analyze and overthink things until the cows come home, I just wanted you to know where my head is at," he said quickly and smiled down at her, kissing her on the forehead before letting her go and going back inside the kitchen.

Tayana stood watching the kitchen door swing back and forth long after he went through it, her mind working a mile a minute. She knew she was a rare breed, things like blood and guts, scattered brain matter, amongst other things, never bothered her in the least, she shook it off and kept it moving. But the look of pain on Jazz's face she saw just a second ago? Shook her to her core.

He was hurt, she could tell, and just what the hell was she going to do now to fix it?

Jazz walked into his bedroom later the same night, naked, proud and erect. Despite the tension from dinner the sight of him made Tayana's mouth water.

She watched him approaching from the center of the bed

where she was completely naked too, holding a metal bowl of ice cubes just as he instructed. The bite of the cold against her skin had chills moving through her body.

"So, Boss Lady, I figured we would play a little bit tonight, you know blow off a little steam," he announced, crawling onto the bed with her, after grabbing the silk scarf she wore earlier. 'Boss Lady', shit, he was still upset with her.

"Now, I want you to lie down on your back and close your eyes," Jazz instructed, grabbing her by the wrists. "Do you trust me, Tayana?" he asked, weaving the ends of the silk scarf through the slats in the headboard.

Tayana nodded slowly, with her eyes closed, wondering what he was up to now. Life in the bedroom with Jazz was never boring or predictable, he was always thinking of new ways to keep her on her toes and begging for more.

Jazz quickly tied her wrists with the silk scarf and picked up an ice cube running it across her lips until they tingled before he licked the water from them. Tayana tried to kiss him and he moved his mouth away from hers.

"For this game I'm going to need you to use your words, Tayana," he stated, dropping the ice cube back into the metal bowl of ice that was still resting between her legs.

He reached over on her side of the bed and held up her sleep mask by the satin ribbons before climbing on top of her, straddling her lap, "So let me ask again and bear in mind how much I hate repeating myself, do you trust me, Tayana?" he asked her, his face set hard, his eyes flashing darkly as he looked down at her tethered to the bed.

"Yes, I trust you, Jazz. Will you tell me what you are about to do before you blindfold me?" Tayana asked, blinking up at him a few times before swallowing nervously. She could tell he was still upset about their conversation earlier and she knew, in her heart of hearts, he would never do anything to hurt her but still, the thought of being tied up and not being able to see made her nervous as hell.

"Aww, come on, Tayana. What does it matter what I'm about to do if you trust me?" Jazz asked, narrowing his eyes at her before he moved forward and placed the mask over her eyes and tied the ribbons tight behind her head.

Reaching back into the bowl he grabbed another piece of ice and trailed it down her lips, across her nipples, down her torso and stopped when he got to her pubic hair, then followed the trail of moisture back up her body with his tongue, taking special care to lick each nipple in turn.

Tayana arched off the bed, moaning softly. Jazz chuckled and pressed her back down on the bed.

"Relax, this game is just getting started," he whispered, moving the bowl of ice from between her legs. He grabbed a piece and dragged it down one of her thighs, to her ankle and her foot and up the opposite one. He even swirled it in her belly button before letting the remainder of the ice cube melt in her pubic hairs, then leaning forward he slowly blew them dry.

"Oh my damn, Jazz," Tayana moaned, pulled against her restraints while moving her hips. One second she was trying to get closer to his mouth the next she was trying to get away from it, the chill of the ice and his warm breath already had her ready to lose it.

He reached up and put his hands on her hips to make her be still again. "Rule number one, you will be still, Tayana. This is an exercise in trust *and* control, my control. I will either reposition you myself or tell you what to do, understand?" Jazz asked blowing on her pubic hairs again.

Tayana nodded her head as an involuntary shiver passed through her body, a biting smack came out of nowhere on her right upper thigh, she had no idea what he hit her with but it wasn't his hand.

"I believe I told you to use your words and no moving," Jazz hissed after repositioning himself so he was close to her ear. She felt his hard dick pressing against her side as he leaned forward and bit her earlobe. "Now, again, do you understand the rules of our little game, Tayana?"

"Yes, I understand," Tayana answered through gritted teeth, she wanted Jazz so bad, her senses were soaring. She heard the rattle of ice so she assumed he was grabbing another piece and sure enough a few seconds later she felt the biting cold of the ice on each one of her nipples in turn followed by Jazz's warm mouth and tongue. The urge to arch her back, to push her breast deeper into his mouth, was almost painful as he repeated the process over and over again.

"Jazz, please," she moaned, the evidence of her arousal wetting the sheets underneath her.

"Please what, Tayana?" he asked pushing one of his ice-cold fingers deep inside of her pussy. "For someone who always has something to say you seem to have a real problem being honest with me and it's really starting to piss me off."

It was amazing how heightened her senses were, not being able to see, every sound and touch seemed amplified. She felt every tug of his mouth on her nipples deep in her saturated opening. His finger moved in and out with slow and deliberate strokes driving Tayana crazy.

She wanted to verbalize exactly what she wanted from him at the moment, but honestly, the slow burn building inside of her had her unable to, so she just moaned his name and fought to keep her body still.

Jazz pulled his finger from inside of her and grabbed another piece of ice, he dragged it from her shoulder down her arm to her fingertips and licked the droplets of water off of each one. Her body was on fire at this point, chill bumps on top of chill bumps were popping up all over her body. Her labored breath seemed louder than she had ever heard it as he moved back down the bed and between her legs.

"Hmmm, since you have nothing to say, I guess it's time to let my mouth to go to work," he said softly, before pressing the piece of ice he had been using to drive her crazy against her quivering clit.

"Oh my damn!" Tayana groaned beginning to tremble all over.

An evil grin spread cross Jazz's face as Tayana whined and gripped the sheets tight as the ice melted against her clit. Her thigh muscles contracted and relaxed as she fought to keep from moving.

He knew, for someone like Tayana, not being in control of her own body was frustrating as hell and after her stubborn ass refused to acknowledge the fact she loved him, it seemed only fitting for her to feel some frustration like he was.

He leaned forward opening her pussy lips and lapped up the melted ice from her wet opening, dragged his tongue up her slit to her clit before sucking on it gently at first, then sucking harder.

The sound that rose from Tayana was a cross between a howl and a whine, as he moved his head from side to side burying his face deeper into her wetness. When his teeth brushed against her clit lightly, her hips came off the bed in a full arch, "Oh shit, Jazz!" she cried out, opening her legs as wide as they would go to give him better access.

He quickly pulled his mouth away, and smacked her twice on each of her upper thighs with the small paddle with holes in it he had looped on his wrist by a leather strap. Like he expected, she was so busy concentrating on him and what he was doing that when he tied her to the bed and put on the blindfold she never noticed it.

"Dammit! What the fuck!" she hissed, as he pushed her hips back down on the bed, he noticed how much wetter she grew immediately.

"Ah, so my beautiful woman can speak, I was beginning to wonder about that. So tell me what could I do right here, right now at this moment to make you happy? I mean I know how much you hate to have your time wasted," he taunted before kissing her in the crease of her inner thigh. Using her words on her actually made him chuckle mischievously.

He leaned forward and licked each of her lower lips. "I'm waiting, Tayana and you know how inpatient I can be," he warned, dragging the paddle down between her legs.

Jazz's dick was painfully hard at this point, he wanted to continue to toy with her but his own hormones were making it hard as hell to think straight and continue the game as well. Her moans and whines echoed around the room as he carried on touching and licking her most intimate parts, he was determined to have her as hot and bothered as she got him, so he grabbed another piece of ice and put it in his mouth, tonguing her opening deep and pushing the ice inside of her pussy.

Tayana's moans became a series of heavy pants as he covered her entire mound with his mouth as the ice melted deep inside of her.

"Shit, no more! Jazz, I need you to fuck me! I need you to fuck me until I forget everything but what's going on in this room right now, please!" she screamed at the top of her voice, drowning out the soft music he had playing in the room.

Jazz alternated moving his mouth and tongue from her clit to her opening, he could tell she was sliding into sexual madness but she wasn't as far gone as he wanted her to be yet.

When he felt her inner walls start to get tight and contract around his tongue, he dragged his mouth away from her and kissed her on her stomach.

"Jazz, what the hell? Please stop doing this to me!" Tayana cried, kicking her legs out full-blown tantrum style.

"When will you learn to listen, woman?" Jazz asked and came up on his knees, flipping her over so she was ass up and brought the paddle down over and over again until her bottom and the back of her thighs were red and splotchy. He watched with a wicked smirk on his face as she began to convulse and jerk just like he wanted her to.

"Omigod. Omigod. Omifuckinggod!" Tayana screamed as her essence poured from deep inside of her and ran down her legs as she came over and over again with torrential force.

Jazz repositioned her shuddering body so she was on her knees and moved behind her sliding on a condom, he put the tip of his dick inside of her overflowing wetness before grabbing her by the hips and slamming his entire length into her roughly.

"Jazz, damn baby!" Tayana sobbed and dropped her head on the mattress as he began to drill his erection deeper and deeper inside of her. He could feel the inside of her vagina still moving from her explosive orgasm and he gripped her hips and went as deep as he could get inside of her.

"I need to feel this forever," he told her gruffly, as he pumped in and out of her in a frenzy, the mixture of passion and frustration was the driving force behind every powerful movement of his hips. She might not allow her lips to say what her yielding body was screaming at him, she was his and would be from now until the end of time.

"Tay, please, for the love of God and all things that make sense, please tell me you didn't just say that Jazz told you he was in love with you and you just stood there saying nothing with a deer in the headlights look on your face!" Yolan demanded moving back to Monet's kitchen to pour herself another drink.

Tayana was sitting on the floor next to Monet's coffee table with her chin resting on the edge of it, looking pitiful. After their 'game' concluded, he untied her and took off the blindfold and gathered her into his arms and reentered her. This time they didn't have sex, they straight up made love. The passion behind his deep and long strokes couldn't be ignored, he used his mouth and his body to make sure there was no doubt of his feelings for her even while she remained unsure.

The next day she called and asked if everyone was free for a girls' night, now here they all sat looking at her like she was the Grinch who stole Christmas or some shit making her feel worse than she already did.

"Yeah, Yo, that is exactly what she just sat here and said she did! What the hell, Whisper? Stevie Wonder can see you love this man, how could you not say it back?" Shay asked, actually pouting, she was all about the happily ever after and damn it, Whisper deserved hers after all she'd been through and done for the entire crew.

Tayana picked up her glass and drained it. Rini's sangria was the best and went amazing with Monet's chicken mole enchiladas which was what they were having for dinner.

"Honestly, don't you think if I knew the real answer to that I would have said it, Shay? So maybe Stevie's ass knows something I just don't yet!" she snapped, checking her phone. Not one new message from Jazz since she sent him their normal good morning text. This was bad, she might have just lost her man!

Moaning pitifully she turned her phone face down on the table and stood up to grab more sangria.

"Honestly, I don't know which is worse, 'I don't know if I like him' Whisper or 'I don't know if I love him' Whisper, but I do know both of you heffas are pitiful as hell!" Monet told her passing her the pitcher of sangria.

Tayana snatched the pitcher off the counter and poured more sangria in her glass. "Hey, hey, hey now, I ain't going to be too many more heffas in this place! Let's not forget I am the freaking boss, ladies!" She slurred, her eyes shining a little bit from the drinks she'd had.

"Then act like it!" All seven of her ladies said almost in unison, and then laughed when they realized what just happened.

"Real talk, we all love you and want nothing but the best for you, but this right here just ain't you! The Tayana we know ain't scared of man, woman, or beast and look at you running like a little punk from a fine ass man, who is your fucking equal in every way, and who, I might add, just told you he's in love with you! Girl Bye! You better woman the hell up and handle this the way Tayana 'Whisper' Bradley handles every goddamn thing, like a muthafucking *boss*!" Yolan snatched the sangria out of her hand and handed her a bottle of water, "No more sangria, you got a call to make."

Chapter 9

"Y ou came highly recommended, Whisper," Slide Savage stated, sitting across from Tayana drinking a glass of Jameson.

"I'm glad to hear that, Mr. Savage. We pride ourselves on the services we provide." Tayana sipped her ginger ale and ran his face through her memory bank, she had seen him recently but couldn't quite place where.

Nonetheless business was business and hers had to continue even though she still hadn't had the heart to heart she wanted to have with Jazz. He had cancelled on her twice now and it had been over three weeks since he told her he loved her, so yeah she had fucked up big time!

They still spoke on the phone daily and even sent text messages but neither one of them was addressing the big issues hanging over their heads and she still had no idea how she really felt.

As always, her ladies were scattered throughout the restaurant sans Monet and Shay, for obvious reasons.

"My people failed to inform me of how breathtaking you

are," Slide stated, taking another gulp from his glass, his eyes centering on her cleavage.

"Because my looks aren't important, how I operate my business is. Now, I am sure you are as busy as I am. Shall we get down to business and your reason for this meeting?" Tayana sat back and waited for Slide to speak, his roaming eyes already getting on her fucking nerves.

"Well, Whisper, I saw the puppets and I'm the type of person who likes to know who is controlling the strings," he said with a smug smile, that Jameson was loosening his tongue a little too much.

"Mr. Savage, before we go any further, I would strongly suggest you refrain from referring to any of my crew in a derogatory manner. If you cannot respect my ladies then I suggest you take your business elsewhere." Tayana took another sip from her glass feeling hostile, she was not feeling his smug ass and wanted to walk away from this bullshit ass meeting already and she had just got there.

"My apologies, I meant no harm, Whisper. That is a sexy ass name by the way. Now, I need to use your cleaning services as soon as possible. I have several items that require attention and as I said, you came highly recommended." Slide reached over and ran his finger across her hand which she quickly removed from the table.

"Fine. Make an appointment with Monet. She can assist you from here on out. As far as the new discoveries from the Motherland, let's see how the dry cleaning goes first." Tayana finished her ginger ale and stood to leave.

"Sounds good, I look forward to working with you and your organization," Slide said, reaching out and running his finger up Tayana's arm.

Tayana smiled and leaned down so she was near Slide's ear. She dropped her arm around his neck and pulled him closer. His eyes lit up at her flash of cleavage just before she pressed Mary Jane deep in his ribs.

"Mr. Savage, that is now twice you have laid an unwelcome finger on me. Might I suggest a refresher course in manners before you set that appointment? None of my ladies appreciate being ogled or touched inappropriately by anyone and, fair warning, some of them are not anywhere near as patient as I am, understand?" Her venomous smile moved slowly across her face as she looked over at him.

Slide swallowed hard and nodded, blinking rapidly in fear. "Understood."

"Great, I look forward to working with you, Mr. Savage, have a great rest of your night, have a little something to eat, it's on me." Tayana winked at him, smiling coldly, and stood up straight and exited the restaurant.

———

Riding home from the restaurant Tayana racked her brain to figure out where she knew Slide from. Khyrs and Jaidyn hadn't brought up much up on him other than three baby mamas and the fact he had moved to Houston two years ago but they were digging deeper. She instructed Monet to stall until they had more intel, there was no way she was going to put her ladies in harm's way.

She looked down at the message she received from Jazz while she was in her meeting with Slide, he told her something majorly important just came up and he was going out of town for the next three days and he promised they would talk when he got back. She closed her eyes and sighed resting her head back against the leather back seat of her town car as Bruise drove her home, immediately Jazz's light eyes and sexy smile moved to the front of her mind, she opened her eyes and stared out of the window shaking her head at her sudden realization as much as she hated to admit it and had resisted, she was in love with Jazz.

She was standing under the scalding hot sprays of the shower anxiously debating on texting Jazz. When she got out of the shower she asked him to Facetime her so they could talk, when suddenly gold bottles of Ace of Spades fluttered across her mind.

"Muthafucka!" she shouted out loud. That is where she had seen Slide before, in the VIP, Jazz's VIP!

This motherfucker put one of his boys on her to see her business' inner workings and leaves town! It was Thirst all over again. Ain't this about a bitch!

Tayana dragged out of bed the next day. She hadn't slept at all. She reached over and grabbed her phone; 27 missed phone calls and 13 text messages, all from Jazz after she sent him the simple text, 'Lose my fucking number'! Fuck him!

"Tay?" Yolan knocked softly on her bedroom door before opening it. Yolan was the first person she called the minute she figured out who Slide was, not her second in command but her best friend. Yolan crossed the room and pulled Tayana in her arms. Silent tears Tayana refused to shed before now slid down her face.

When her crying jag was over, Yolan pulled her from her embrace and looked at her. "Tay, I won't ask if you are okay, because I know you're not. But I have to ask what you are going to hate me for asking." She warned, wincing at Tayana.

Tayana wiped her face and looked at Yolan, the one who knew her better than anyone else did, her 'A1 from Day One'.

"What's up, Yo? You know I could never hate you," Tayana told her, reaching over and grabbing a tissue from the box on her bedside table, several discarded ones already rested next to it, she had been crying her eyes out all night.

"Have you even talked to Jazz to hear his side of things, Tay?" Yolan asked her calmly, taking the tissue from Tayana's hand and wiping away her best friend's tears.

Tayana rolled her eyes in Yolan's direction then silently glared at her bedroom wall.

"I knew it! Tay, you have to talk to the man. Listen to his side of things. You know good and damn well if we find out he facilitated this shit, he's a dead man but before we kill the love of your life, make sure he deserves to die," Yolan reasoned and took both of Tayana's hands, pleading with her.

"He's out of town, Yo! I can't do this over the phone. I have to see him when I talk to him, read his body language," she explained quietly biting the inside of her cheek, she felt so fucking stupid!

Yolan shook her head. "I know you, Tay, and you know he's genuinely in love with you. You're spooked because you're in love with him too. The man could break your nail by accident and that would be a reason to leave him right now."

Tayana snatched her hands away and flung herself off the bed seeing red.

"This ain't just a broken fucking nail Yo! I saw Slide in Jazz's VIP. I saw him, Yolan. You know if I'm telling you I saw him, then I saw him!" she ranted, fuck what Yolan was talking about. None of that shit mattered now, this was about Jazz's ass being shady as fuck!

Yolan leaned on Tayana's pillows and shrugged. "Then why haven't you sounded the alarm, *Whisper*?" Yolan asked quietly, pulling her gun, a white, mother of pearl handled .357 she called 'Angel' from the holster at the small of her back and laying it on the bed "Call it so we can put this chapter of bull-shit to rest."

Tayana stopped pacing and looked over at Yolan in surprise. She had never called her 'Whisper' before in her life, as a matter of fact she refused to. Yolan could have slapped the shit out of her and she wouldn't be more shocked by that than she was right now.

Tayana's face crumbled as she sank to the ground. "Because I love him, Yo. I love him, and if he did this, I don't know what to do!" she sobbed covering her face. "For the first time in like forever, I don't know what to do!"

Yolan re-holstered Angel and led Tayana back to the bed. "Don't trip, if he did this your ladies are murking his ass, so you don't have to do anything. Until then get some rest and let the lethals do what we do," Yolan told her, pulling her phone out and walking out of her room leaving Tayana to her pitiful thoughts.

Tayana sat in her office at the gallery, staring at the three prints Jazz had ordered, four days later. She had been radio silent even after he got back to Houston. She logged onto her computer and sent him an email that said she would deliver his prints at 7:00 pm if that worked for him. 'See you then' was all he replied. He had stopped calling and texting two days ago.

She closed her eyes and took a long cleansing breath before packaging the prints. She had Bruise drive her Land Rover over so she could handle this alone, for now. She was still waiting for more intel on Slide hoping that for once she was wrong and he just happened to be in Jazz's VIP as a visitor.

Just as she pulled into Jazz's driveway, her phone rang. She accepted the call and held the phone to her ear silently.

"Whisper, Slide was a corner boy for 'Heavy' back in the day, part of one of the crews we phased out when we took over," Jaidyn stated.

"Have Monet arrange a meeting. Looks like his clothing was damaged at the cleaners," Tayana ordered, hung up and watched as Jazz walked down the driveway to the back of her Rover.

Tayana popped the hatch and slid out of the driver's seat, dressed in all black. Her hair pulled back in a tight ponytail. Mary Jane was at the small of her back instead of her usual ankle holster just in case.

Jazz silently watched her approach and pulled out two of the three framed prints. He waited to make sure she could handle the last one before turning and heading back to the house.

The great room was empty so she assumed he had taken the print to the office. She made her way to his office and found him sitting in his high-backed chair, the prints were resting next to the first one.

"So what's up, Boss Lady?" Jazz sneered at her. His icy glare stopped her in her tracks. She sighed in defeat shaking her head, he acted like this was easy for her, like this was business as usual, she loved him but if what she suspected was true then he couldn't be trusted and this thing between them was over.

"Jazz, I just came to deliver and hang the prints as per the 'Essie's guarantee'," she said, dropping her gaze and concentrating on unwrapping the three new prints.

Jazz sat up in his chair, leaned on the desk looking incredulous.

"I don't give a *fuck* about these prints. Do you have any

fucking idea what I've been through in the past month? Some sick shit went down in one of my operations and I got taken for $500,000, some idiot with a death wish set my mom's car on fire and I leave town to handle that shit and get her moved to a safer place to come back to your ass giving me the silent treatment after I told you I was in love with you, you say *nothing* back and then you try to set up meetings to discuss it like it's a business transaction and not a fucking relationship! With all the shit going down around me I was actually afraid someone had managed to get to you and was using your phone to draw me out, I thought you were hurt, Tayana. I had my guys at all of your businesses looking for you!" he snapped, sitting back hard.

"Was Slide one of the ones you sent to look for me or is he just one of your undercovers?" Tayana asked, glaring back at him, he wasn't going to make her the only bad guy here!

"What the fuck does it matter who I sent? And what the fuck are you talking about, 'undercover'?" Jazz demanded, his jaw jumped angrily.

"He's been with you about 15 years, right? Moved to Houston two years ago?" Tayana asked, ignoring his questions, feeling the burn of tears that wanted to fall, fuck this hurt to even hint to what she believed was going on, but she had to know the truth.

"Yeah, something like that. Now why the fuck are we talking about Slide? We are talking about me and you, that was some foul shit you pulled, Boss Lady." Jazz looked like he hadn't slept in days, he had stubble from not shaving. He was in a pair of Levi's and a non-brand t-shirt.

"We are talking about Slide because you sent him to my operation to clean money that's why," Tayana said quietly sitting in the chair directly across from him, wiping away the few stray tears that fell from her eyes.

Jazz considered what she said rubbing his chin. As realization hit, his eyes darkened and his face was deadly. "I didn't send Slide or anybody else to you to wash shit, Whisper. Why the fuck would I do that? I wash my own money."

Tayana let out the breath she had been holding in. "He's asking us to clean 10 mil."

"I will handle his ass. Now is that the reason for this silent shit you pulled?" Jazz asked, looking into her eyes still looking cold and deadly.

Tayana held his gaze. "Yes, Jazz that's why. I couldn't have this conversation over the phone. I had to know the truth."

Jazz stood up and leaned on the desk. "Wow. And now that you know the truth what happens? What happens now, Boss Lady?"

Tayana looked at him. "I honestly don't know, Jazz." She never thought past confronting him about Slide or anything else, she had let her emotions lead.

Jazz scoffed and moved around the desk and walked to the office door. "Well, here's what I know, I paid over $100,000 to your gallery for these prints, I'd like them hung. When that's done, our business with each other is too. The last thing I need in my life is the woman I love, and thought I wanted to spend the rest of my life with, to not trust me. Good night, Boss Lady."

Tayana looked over her shoulder at his retreating back. She noticed he had some tools on the edge of the desk and a tall step stool set out for her to hang the prints. She wiped away more tears and got to work, the sooner she got this done the sooner she could put this entire thing with Jazz behind her, at least that was what sounded good in her heartbroken mind.

Since Jazz wasn't there to consult, she hung each. The male print on the right wall, the woman on the left and the last two in the center.

After making sure they were secure and properly hung, Tayana sank into Jazz's desk chair making sure they worked in the room the way they were positioned.

She pulled her phone out of her back pocket. "Yo, I fucked up, bad. He hates me," she whined, trying not to start crying again.

Tayana sat back in the desk chair staring up at the ceiling.

"Fuck that, Tay, that's a cop-out. He's hurt, woman up and fix it and don't come home until you do," Yolan snapped and hung up.

Tayana pulled her phone from her ear, closed her eyes and screamed into her hands. "Are you fucking kidding me, Yo!" She didn't know what the fuck to do, she wasn't the apologetic, please forgive me type.

As soon as that thought crossed her mind, she could almost hear Yolan telling her, "Well if you want your man back, you are today, Heffa!"

This was going to be hard. She had never genuinely apologized to another person in her life, seemed fitting it would be to the man she loved.

Tayana stood at the bottom of the mahogany staircase actually trembling with fear. "Come on, Tayana, you can do this, just put one foot in front of the other," she told herself out loud.

"Jazz?" she called up the stairs, biting the inside of her cheek while she waited.

When he didn't answer, she moved halfway up the staircase and called out louder. "Jazz!" Still no answer, she felt herself getting annoyed but took a deep breath and moved to the top of the staircase. "Jazz!"

Now she was no longer nervous, she figured he was ignoring her and moved into the hallway that led to his room determined to have it out with him, good or bad outcome at least she tried to fix it. Yolan had to give her credit for that. To her relief she heard the shower in his bedroom running; he wasn't ignoring her, he just didn't hear her calling him.

Tayana paused at the closed bedroom door before opening it, and crossing to the open bathroom door where steam was billowing out. Her breath caught in her chest.

Jazz was standing in the middle of his two-door shower, sprays from both sides and top shower heads rained down on him, he stood staring at her through the water running down his face like he'd been waiting for her.

Tayana stood in the doorway mesmerized. His golden skin glistened in the water, droplets of water ran down his muscular chest and pooled around his growing erection.

Jazz tapped the glass on one of the doors and it swung open. He continued to stand in the middle of the spray staring at her.

Tayana pulled Mary Jane from the small of her back and put the gun on the chair closest to her, she slipped her black Chanel booties off and unbuttoned her silk blouse sliding it off her shoulders slowly. Her bra soon followed. Her eyes never left his. He licked his lips as she peeled her jeans down her legs and stepped into the steamy bathroom wearing only a silk thong.

"Jazz, I have to say this before I come in that shower or I never will," she told him while messing with her platinum bracelet with nine interlocking hearts on it symbolizing her and her ladies, including Asia, they all had one.

A pained look crossed his face for a moment before he nodded.

"Okay." Water still ran down his face, his dick was like a homing beacon; it was pointed straight out and seemed to move where she moved.

"Jazz, I'm sorry. I'm sorry for what I put you through and most of all, I am sorry for not trusting you. I said it before with my mouth, this time I'm saying it with my heart. Jazz, I trust you and I love you. I love you and I am so in love with you it's driving me insane! I know I hurt you but I promise you if you give me just one more chance it will never happen again. You are my equal in every way and I want to spend the rest of my life with you," Tayana said nervously and watched his face for a reaction. For several seconds, he was silent, still staring at her.

"Are you finished?" he asked quietly, bracing his arms on the walls moving his head out of the water falling from above.

Tayana's eyes narrowed. She had just poured her heart out to his ass and his response was, 'are you finished'! "Yeah, I'm finished," she snapped, throwing attitude.

"Finally! Took you long enough. Shit! And after what you just put me through, check that attitude, you have no right to have one," Jazz snapped as he reached out, snatched her into the shower, and smacked her on the ass, before pinning her against the wall and kissing her fiercely.

She threw her arms around his neck as he hooked his finger in the elastic of her thong and pulled, ripping it off. He picked her up and guided himself inside of her. She locked her legs around his waist and used his shoulders for leverage as she began to move up and down on his rock-hard dick.

He grabbed her hips bringing her down even harder, pressing her back solidly against the wall, he let go of one of her hips and leaned down and captured her breast in his mouth.

"Fuck! I missed you, baby! You pull some shit like that again, I'm finding your ass and dragging you back here by your fucking hair and believe me, Tayana, your security ain't enough to stop me either," he growled in her ear right before he bit it.

Tayana bounced up and down on his erection, refusing to come because if she came, he came. "I know, baby, and I'm sorry Jazz, I love you, baby! I love you." She panted as her orgasm tried to claw its way free but she fought to hold on just a little bit longer.

Jazz gripped her by the ass and drove himself even deeper. His erection grew about to burst, stretching her walls. He slammed into her hard as he began to come. "I love you, too, Tayana. I love you, too."

As he made his declaration of love, she finally allowed herself to come too.

"Jazz?" Tayana was laying on top of Jazz barely able to move after round three in the shower. Her tight ponytail was a thing of the past, her natural hair down and curly from the humidity and moisture from the shower and their make-up sex.

Jazz was idly running his fingers up and down her freshly lotioned back. "Yes, Tayana?" He answered her with his eyes closed, he was on his way to sleep until she called his name.

"I know this is not the time to talk about this but I think you ought to know, Slide used to work for Heavy. For that alone, I should want his head but he disrespected my ladies and moreover, he disrespected me," she informed him basically letting him know she wanted to handle his ass.

Jazz sighed, looking down at Tayana. "Baby, you heard me, I will handle Slide," he told her, kissing her on the forehead. "You said you trust me, then trust your man, Boss Lady," he snapped, smacking her on her ass. Damn she really loved when he did that!

"I heard you, Jazz, and I trust you one-hundred percent, but that muthafucka is grimy! Should have opened his ass up when he touched me, the bastard!" Tayana mumbled fiercely, still laying on top of Jazz's chest.

Jazz sat up, making her lift up too, looking down at her

indignantly, "Dafuq you mean he touched you?" he demanded, his eyes were cold and squinted in anger..

Tayana actually shrank back a little. "Relax, Jazz, I set his ass straight, you know how I get down," she reasoned, touching his face hoping to calm him down.

Jazz took her hand, kissed her palm, lay back down and pulled her close again. "Change of plans, I know you're not one to compromise but I believe we need to collab just this once."

Tayana's eyes were getting heavy, she listened to the calming rhythm of his heartbeat. "Cool," she muttered as her eyes closed.

Chapter 10

"So what's up with my money, Whisper? I thought you would have been done by now," Slide asked, taking a blunt from behind his ear and lighting it in the frame room in the gallery.

"We would have been done had we known about the watermark. That has to be done through completely different channels and raises the cost," Tayana stated calmly, as Jaidyn walked over and snatched the blunt from his mouth.

"Strike one," she told him, walking a little closer to him, her hands clasped together calmly in front of her.

"Fuck you mean raises the cost? What watermark? I know your stuck-up ass ain't trying to get over on me!" Slide snapped, shooting daggers at Jaidyn, who was standing closer to him than Tayana and had her baby 9mm, 'Bella', tucked at her side.

"There is a watermark on the bills other than the ones from the United States Government so none of our local channels will touch it. I will have to have it cleaned internationally. The price to do that is 1.5 million," she told him with a sympathetic smile.

Slide sputtered indignantly. "1.5 million? I should have known that your bitch ass would be as crooked as your fucking daddy!" he shouted trying to move closer to Tayana.

Jaidyn stepped between them and punched him in the mouth, knocking out two of his front teeth. "Strike two," Tayana said calmly with a sigh.

"Man, fuck you, Whisper! Fuck you! Fuck you! What are you even talking about? What watermark? Your bitch ass just dirty! I should drop this little bitch here and shove my dick down your throat, teach your ass a woman's place!" Slide shouted, spitting out blood on the cement floor.

Tayana pulled Mary Jane from the small of her back and cocked her. She ached to pull the trigger right then. This pencil dick, weak tooth having bastard had crossed the fucking line but she promised Jazz she would let him take out Slide, so she moved her finger away from the trigger.

Jazz stepped in the room with his 9mm with a silencer, dressed to kill literally. His black suit, midnight blue shirt and tie, and black loafers made him look dangerous and deadly to anyone he came up against at the moment and completely sexy and fuckable to Tayana. She fought hard as hell to keep the 'That's *my* man' smile off of her face.

"Damn, Slide you let a tiny ass female like that knock you to your knees?"

Jazz's light eyes were cold as steel. Slide's eyes grew in fear knowing his thieving ass was caught.

"Yo, Jazz! I don't know what these bitches told you but I'm out here trying to grow our shit using my own money and they trying to strong arm me and shit," Slide explained quickly, blood still coming from his mouth.

A cold smile crept on Jazz's face. "Slide, you have been with me fifteen years. I want to believe you, I really do, but there are two things stopping me, bruh."

Jaidyn handed Jazz a hundred-dollar bill that he held up to the light, he shook his head sadly and sighed.

"The fact your dumb ass is trying to wash the same exact amount that came up missing in the last two months and it has my watermark." Jazz shook his head sadly.

"Strike three," Tayana said with a poisonous smile as she shot Slide in the groin and walked out of the room, tucking Mary Jane back into her waist band as she went.

Jazz walked out a minute later, unscrewing his silencer. Handing both to his buff, security guard who actually made Jazz look small. The man looked like a wall with feet.

"Your place, my cleaner?" Jazz asked, walking up to her after sending the human wall back to his car.

"No, my place, my cleaner. One day your people will be on my people's level," Tayana teased, chucking her chin at her clean up crew's direction as they rushed in to clean up. Jaidyn had already taken the back way up to the gallery showroom.

Jazz shook his head, looking down at her and reached into his jacket's inside breast pocket. "Damn, I love you. Marry me, Tayana." He dropped to one knee and pulled out a custom, one of a kind six-carat princess cut diamond and platinum ring out of the ring box in his hand.

"I love you too, Jazz," she choked out through her sudden onslaught of tears, nodding as he slid the engagement ring on her finger before standing up and kissing her deeply.

She noticed him looking over her shoulder when they broke apart and turned around to find all eight of her lethals, including Asia aka Neutral, standing in the shadows near the elevator watching them. All eight were smiling, Joy's just wasn't as bright as the other seven ladies.

"Do you think your girl Joy will ever take the target off my back?" he whispered in her ear before nipping it and looking over at her crew again.

Tayana looked from her ladies and back up at him smiling evilly, "Probably not, my ladies don't play when it comes to 'Boss Lady'." She smirked before kissing him again.

Epilogue

One Year Later

Jazz and Tayana had joined forces and were holding down Houston and slowly moving into Dallas and Austin. They were slowly moving out of all of their illegal operations and ran their businesses like a well-oiled machine.

Tayana pointed out the weaknesses she noticed in his crew, that was one part of the business Jazz relented and admitted she and her ladies were more on top of things than he was and he merged his security with hers, Joy and Rini quickly cleaned up and weeded out the weak or questionable ones on his team and those who remained where hired by The Firm. Now, The Firm protected them all.

At first sharing control and having someone challenge Tayana on her decisions sometimes was hard but with a man like Jazz by her side, she was learning to accept it. Yolan had been right on the money, he was her equal in every way and it was hard to believe her need to always be in control almost pushed him completely out of her life.

Tayana stood with her back to the crashing waves of the Atlantic ocean on the beach in front of Jazz's house in the Bahamas. The occasional cool spray of water danced on her shoulders then ran down her back in tiny trails.

The hem of her ivory lace Vera Wang gown was wet from the spray. She held hands with her husband of one week as they recited their vows in front of their family.

To appease Jazz's mother and her new mother-in-law, Alice, they had a traditional church wedding at his mother's home church in Georgia the week before. Neither Alice nor Jazz knew most of the people there besides 'the church ladies' as he called them but nonetheless, the church was filled to capacity. With Alice's stamp of approval, they donated most of the wedding gifts they received from the congregation to a battered women and children's shelter, not because they were ungrateful but because they wanted to give back to the poor community there.

Jazz, who was wearing a Stuart Hughes white suit and Santoni shoes, kept looking down at the waves threateningly as they got closer and closer to his custom shoes.

"Jazz, stop tripping. Nobody told you to wear leather shoes to the beach in the first damn place, Mr. Clothes Whore," Tayana whispered fiercely. He glared at her as the preacher cleared her throat.

"If there are no objections, I now pronounce you, Mr. and Mrs. Jazz Jones. You may now kis-"

"Hold up! Hold up! We now pronounce you, Mr. and Mrs. Jazz Jones, the heavy hittas of H-Town!" Yolan shouted with tears of happiness filling her eyes. "Tay, it took your ass long enough to get your shit together!"

Jazz threw her a maddening look. "Okay, Yo we know she is a stubborn, hardheaded, pain in the ass but can I kiss her now?" he asked as he pulled Tayana into his arms and softly kissed her lips. "I love you, Tayana, Whisper, Boss Lady, Bradley Jones."

Tayana looked around at all her ladies, all loved, all standing on their own, all happy for her before looking up at Jazz with tears of happiness ruining her makeup. "I love you too, Jazz 'Boss Man' Jones," she teased.

Her crew circled her, each hugging her in turn before allowing Jazz into the circle and their lives forever.

The End

Joy Bussu

Blessings! I am 48-year-old Joy Bussu. Eighteen years married, mother of four, grandmother of one. I was born in Wichita Falls, Texas, but raised in Denver, Colorado, where I currently reside with my beautiful family.

I have always had a love for the written word. I devoured books from the time I could string sentences together and I have always loved to write. Once I gave birth to my youngest child and only daughter, I was finally ready to attempt to write my first book. It took me over ten years to complete it.

Holding the first copy of my self-published book was the opening of the flood gate I never even realized I was holding back. Writing is my passion and my life and it is my pleasure and deepest honor to be able to share it with the world. My dream is to touch as many as humanly possible with my work.

Visit my webpage

Don't miss these exciting titles by Joy Bussu and Blushing Books!

Dangerous Love series
The Art of Love

Nieko's Treasure
Whispers
Makia's Bodyguard

Anthologies
12 Naughty Days of Christmas 2020

Blushing Books

Blushing Books is the oldest eBook publisher on the web. We've been running websites that publish steamy romance and erotica since 1999, and we have been selling eBooks since 2003. We have free and promotional offerings that change weekly, so please do visit us at http://www.blushingbooks.com/free.

Blushing Books Newsletter

Please join the Blushing Books newsletter
to receive updates & special promotional offers.
You can also join by using your mobile phone:
Just text BLUSHING to 22828.

Every month, one new sign up via text messaging will receive
a $25.00 Amazon gift card, so sign up today!